Born in London, Janice Gold is presently living in Hertfordshire where initially she had opened a small ladies wear boutique. Always interested in art and design, she designed bespoke hats and fascinators for her then clientele. For the past fifteen years she has been part of the Visitor Services team, welcoming visitors to 'Henry Moore Studios & Gardens', the home of sculptor Henry Moore in Perry Green, Hertfordshire. As a dedicated bibliophile, she has combined her love of literature and art to produce this, her first book.

To my dear mum, sister Roz and brother in law Lawrence for your constant support and belief in my abilities. And to the men in my life, my sons, Daniel and Simon, love always.

Janice Gold

THE KISS

AUSTIN MACAULEY PUBLISHERS™

LONDON ∗ CAMBRIDGE ∗ NEW YORK ∗ SHARJAH

A CIP catalogue record for this title is available from the British Library.

ISBN 9781398484184 (Paperback)
ISBN 9781398484191 (ePub e-book)

www.austinmacauley.com

First Published 2023
Austin Macauley Publishers Ltd®
1 Canada Square
Canary Wharf
London
E14 5AA

My upmost thanks go to the Belvedere Museum, Vienna, Austria who unwittingly gave me the inspiration to write this book after visiting and seeing their Klimt collection in person.

Table of Contents

Prologue

31 December 1999

Dear Viktor,

I hope this farewell letter will find you in good health. I am writing it to thank you for introducing me to a life I would never have known. If it hadn't been for you and your foresight, I would never have found the true love of my life.

Your belief in my capabilities never floundered and your trust in me never faltered. I want to thank you also for dismissing my constant doubts as poppycock, when there seemed to be an enormous mountain for me to climb.

I had never known my real grandfather as he had died before I had been born. But I want you to know that in my heart, you have filled that void and have become my own surrogate grandpa; someone I could trust and rely on to speak the truth at all times and to give me much needed advice when I had requested it.

I am going to miss you enormously. But take great comfort when I tell you that as from now, I will become the person I always imagined I would be and fulfil all my dreams and desires. Never more will I lead a mundane existence, as the latter half of 1999 became truly magical in every sense of the word. Instead, I will be forever free of this life's conventional trappings.

Once again, dear Viktor, a big thank you for all that you and your kind family have done for me. Who knows, perhaps one day we *will* meet again? Until then this must be 'Auf Wiederschauen'.

Your dear friend,
Emma Louise Fogle

Chapter One

Vienna, 30 December 1999

Standing transfixed in front of such an iconic painting, Emma trembled, mesmerised by the brilliance and decadence of gold vying with platinum and interspersed with dashes of silver. Gustav Klimt's, *The Kiss*, the real, the actual oil masterpiece and she, Emma Louise Fogle, here witnessing this joyful collaboration of artistry at its finest.

Goodness, how long have I been here? she wondered as she was now aware of a group of visitors being ushered out by a gallery assistant eager for his evening meal.

It must be closing time and I've been here most of the afternoon, she thought to herself.

Surrounded by Klimt's paintings, she had been so enthralled that time had become non-existent. All she had wanted and needed was to be part of Klimt's world. She knew she had become besotted and somehow connected with the subjects involved; the models, the lovers that had entwined themselves in ecstasy. She imagined herself as being that young woman and being caressed with her head held lovingly waiting for that kiss from the dark, mysterious prince of a man dressed in such opulence.

She had been studying all the Klimt paintings The Belvedere had to offer, this being the largest collection of his works and in Vienna, his place of birth. Out of all of them, it was *The Kiss (Loving Couple)* that held her imagination and drew her back repeatedly. Conjuring up in her mind the story it portrayed and comparing it to her solitary existence. *Perhaps, one day, that'll be me being lovingly held in the strong, masculine arms of a handsome man and not wanting to be released.* She sighed feeling elated but also downcast as she knew that was only typical of fairy tales and not true to life.

It had been suggested to Emma that it would benefit her progress in The Hadley Gallery for her to come to Vienna for three weeks to study as many of the Master's works as she was able to. They were training her to be accomplished around Klimt's sketches and lithographs so that she will feel confident when dealing with influential and affluent clientele.

She was instructed to study the techniques he used in his paintings; the brushstrokes and application of oils and other mediums which his artworks are famous for. This opportunity was too good to be true. She felt privileged as she never imagined herself ever being given this chance to apply and better herself. A three-week student entrance pass had been issued by her employer and allocated to her once she had arrived at The Belvedere Museum so that she didn't have that expense to concern herself with.

Unfortunately, her magical time in Vienna was coming to an end. She had spent every day here, studying, making numerous notes and even sketching, although this wasn't her forte. Tomorrow was New Year's Eve, the year 2000 and she would be back regardless to celebrate the start of a new century, albeit a whole new millennium, just her and her favourite masterpiece. Emma shivered as though she knew something significant would be happening. The Belvedere had invited her to the New Year's Eve party they had been preparing for all week. That would be her chance to see *her* painting one more time.

She gave a huge sigh and then reluctantly she followed the last of the stragglers as they made their way out of the gallery and then through another adjoining room full of wondrous paintings that she felt she had neglected to look at; by other renowned artists but her remit was for Klimt only. She was being swiftly corralled down the wide, marble staircase into the entrance hall and foyer, which at that moment resembled a holding pen.

Out into the late afternoon Viennese air, The Belvedere, an imposing, magnificent, Baroque Palace housing a wealth of illustrious art, stood framed by the early evening winter sunset. Silhouetted against the streaked magenta sky, Emma imagined it resembled a scene from a biblical film and she almost expected the voice of God to boom out with a warning as if she had been trespassing. She took one last look at this tableau before hurrying to the exit and onto the busy street. She made her way to the tram stop which she was hoping was the correct one, as she had still not yet fully grasped much of the local language but just a smattering of the words that were useful to her while staying in Vienna.

It was bitter cold and had been snowing most of the night; forming a hard icy surface that glistened under the street lights like a shimmer of magical fairy dust.

At the beginning of December, on almost every street corner, there had suddenly appeared traditional mini-Christmas markets, selling hot dogs and warming, fragrant glühwein as well as snow globes, sparkling angels and hand-made Christmas tree ornaments, all to attract residents and visitors alike. *It had truly become an enchanted city and definitely the best time of the year to be staying here,* Emma thought to herself and revelled in her good fortune as she carefully tried to walk without slipping over.

Her rented apartment in a boarding house was across the city in a lesser-known area called Josefstadt in the 8th district and away from the main tourist spots which was, therefore, substantially more affordable. Although the London-based gallery she worked for had given her an allowance for this 'fact-finding, learn all about Klimt sojourn', she felt they hadn't taken into account the temptations the city's food had to offer. She was unable to resist passing by the enticing pastry houses where the array of the most mouth-watering, delicately piped whipped cream pastries in pastel shades were on display. Her absolute favourite though was apple strudel with cinnamon accompanied with a serving of crème patisserie. It brought back memories of the cake she had first tasted all those months ago at Viktor Bloom's house, but without the cream.

Emma had only joined The Hadley Gallery, an independent art gallery based in Covent Garden, London, as a trainee buyer/evaluator five months ago. When she had gone for the interview, she didn't think she had a hope in hell's chance of getting it. Travelling on the tube to Covent Garden from Ruislip gave her extra time to swat up on the possible questions that might be thrown at her. She knew she had to be a good actress and be persuasive as all she had to offer was an 'A' level in art history which she had gained at her local grammar school, St Mary's Grammar School for Girls. The interview had gone better than she could have hoped for. Both the Hadley brothers, Charles, the eldest and Dominic, the considerably younger one, were present. Rather officious but polite, Charles Hadley seemed to be more assertive and adopted the habit of finishing his brother's sentences. Emma had found this slightly disconcerting, likening it to a tennis match when it reached deuce. So, when they both agreed in unison to appoint her on a three-month trial, she fervently shook their hands. Game, set and match to her.

What seemed to be in her favour, she felt, was the fact that Charles' daughter, Helena, had also been an alumna of St Mary's and had achieved great kudos as head girl the previous year. Emma had left school four years ago, so their paths had never crossed; but from the description she had been given at the interview, she had the feeling, call it instinct perhaps, that his Helena was a high achiever, intent at such a young age to crash glass ceilings in the near future with an almighty sledge hammer.

Although Emma knew herself to be a confident, gregarious young woman, she did feel slightly unnerved knowing she'll have to be liaising part of the working week alongside Uncle Dominic's ambitious niece, who was brought in to learn the family business.

"Just a minute," Emma admonished herself. "I've had relevant working experience which must go in my favour."

For just over a year, she had been employed by a small, independent art gallery in Cambridge, prestigiously opposite King's College and situated in prime position on King's Parade. It had become too expensive for her to live there in the end as the rent had been quite steep. Even by her living on the perimeter of the city and cycling in every day, still only gave her a pittance to juggle with for any of life's essentials, such as food or heaven *forbid,* a new pair of shoes. She had felt returning to London, well Ruislip, had been the right decision. Even though it had meant briefly, fingers crossed, living back home with her mum; sadly, her father had died suddenly two years ago from an embolism to his brain and that had left her mother living on her own. Emma had only then just applied for the position in Cambridge and had felt guilty leaving her mum alone but she had insisted that she should still go. But now, she needed to establish herself by acquiring a decent salary in hopefully a decent company with decent prospects. She hoped that The Hadley Gallery would be the one for her to be able to achieve all of that.

Chapter Two

Covent Garden, London

During her three-month trial period, Emma knew she had to work hard to prove that she was going to be an asset to The Hadley. She was almost at the end now and enjoying the intenseness of studying the various bibliographies and catalogue raisonné of the artists' works currently in their possession. Often, she went home late in the evening with a pounding headache for forgetting to take a lunch break as she'd been so engrossed in searching for a particular document to help prove provenance on a client's prized painting or sketch.

While she was absorbed in completing that day's assignment, Emma was aware that Dominic had entered her small office in the basement of the building. She had been slightly disappointed at first when she had been shown this tiny room as it felt cramped with books and boxes stacked high, blocking out any natural light the dirt-ingrained window tried to offer. He hovered looking over her shoulder, inspecting the notes she had made. She felt herself blushing as she was aware of the intoxicating, citrus scent of his aftershave surrounding her; fortunately, she had her head down, so he hadn't witnessed her embarrassment.

"I hope I'm not disturbing you, Emma, as I can see you seem to be totally engaged in your work, but I thought you might like a break from it for a while." He suggested kindly. "I'm just popping out to visit a new client and feel it would be beneficial for you to accompany me. Are you in agreement?"

"Of course, I would love to. It will give me valuable experience and a wonderful excuse to get some fresh air and stretch my legs." She said cheekily. He smiled at her knowingly as he knew it was a dig at the undesirable room she had been allocated. He will definitely rectify this as soon as she becomes a permanent member of their team, which he had an instinct she will be soon. Although she hadn't been with the gallery for long-roughly ten weeks, he could see how eager she had become in that short time; quite capable and with a brilliant eye for detail.

He helped her on with her jacket. Thankfully, that morning she had decided to wear the smarter of the two she owned-the dark navy one with white piping round the pocket flaps. This was her standard interview attire which she regularly alternated with either navy or white trousers. *How fortuitous*, she thought to herself, that she chose right; she must have had an inkling that today was going to be special and that she would be required to look the part of the young, ambitious art gallery, evaluator/buyer she felt she could be.

Helena was in the main gallery assisting her father, Charles, with hanging new art pieces that had recently been shipped over from Europe, when they both walked through together. Charles enjoyed this aspect of gallery life as it gave him a chance to reconnect with the past when the gallery was first opened. He made a point of overseeing the new artists' works they had acquired and to display them in a prominent area where they could be viewed from the street through the strengthened, plate glass window and catch the eye of any discerning art collector. Charles was in his late forties and had opened The Hadley when he was thirty-three. This was relatively young to be able to acquire premises in such a prestigious part of the city. Their father had died suddenly from a stroke which had been a shock to them as he had lived a fairly healthy life; drinking alcohol only at weekends and regular trips to the gym. This had made Charles determined to succeed in his life and live it to the full. Their father had left both him and Dominic an inheritance, not a great fortune but enough to use as a deposit to start a business with should they wish to do so. Charles had always had an avid interest in the art world, and so he had visited other independent art galleries and auction houses many times to give him credence and knowledge before opening The Hadley. Dominic had come on board as a partner when he was twenty-seven and ready to become an entrepreneur and take on responsibilities. They worked well together and built on the goodwill and reputation of being an honest, ethical and reliable establishment.

Dominic called out to Charles as they were leaving and stepping out into the quiet, mid-morning street, "I have a lead that might prove interesting. An elderly gentleman called this morning about a Klimt sketch he has in his possession and would like it to be authenticated. I'm taking Emma along with me as it'll be good experience for her. Shan't be too long and she'll be back in her little cubby-hole before you can shake a tail feather."

Cheek, Emma thought to herself indignantly. *He regards me like a budgerigar to be put back in my cage after a short flight out. Still, I'll prove what an asset I'll be to him and Charles, then I'll make him eat his words along with some bird seed perhaps.* With this thought in her mind, she giggled to herself and hurried to catch him up as he was descending into the staff car park below their building.

"Why can't I go with Uncle Dominic to visit that person?" Helena whined. "I'm also supposed to be learning all about the business. I should take priority as one day I'll be, as your daughter and heir, heading the company once you and Uncle Dominic are too old."

Charles was surprised by the vitriol in Helena's voice and saddened to realise this is how she really felt.

"My darling, Helena, you shouldn't feel neglected and taken for granted because you are important to us as a family member entering the business. We need you to learn every aspect of gallery life which means starting at the very bottom. You're only eighteen, so be patient."

Feeling disgruntled by her father's admonishment, Helena threw the bronze maquette back into its crate and stormed off. Luckily, the crate was full of straw, so Charles could see no damage had been done to it, otherwise it would have proved an expensive tantrum.

She hurried to the front of the gallery and looked through the window as Dominic's silver Mercedes accelerated up the slope of the car park and into the road. She could see they were laughing, possibly at something witty her uncle had said. It made her feel so young and insignificant. Not a good feeling and definitely not a feeling she was used to.

Helena was the only child of Sadie, Charles' second wife when they had met at a mutual friend's dinner party. He knew it had been arranged as a blind date for both of them but the match making had proved a success, as only a year later, they were married. Helena had been only five years old as a bridesmaid at their wedding and even then, she stole the limelight with her precocious deliverance of a song and tap dance routine. Loved and spoilt by them both, they indulged her to such a degree that she was oblivious to other people's feelings. Charles had never had any children with his first wife as that marriage had lasted barely a year before divorce proceedings began. Consequently, he lavished his affections and money on making Helena happy, believing this would give her the confidence she would need to succeed in the future. So now, she strongly concluded, that it was her birth right to forge her way ahead, regardless of whose toes she needed to step on and felt the power from her own perfectly pedicured feet encased in smart, indecently expensive Christian Louboutin shoes to take her there.

Chapter Three

October 1999, Mr Bloom

As she got into his car, Emma sank into the plush, cream, soft leather upholstery of the passenger seat; such luxury, like being in a bath of whipped cream. Not that she had ever had that experience and so blushed thinking of the possibilities.

She realised Dominic had been talking to her and was waiting for a reply.

"Sorry, I was miles away, what did you say?" she apologised.

"I was asking you if you are settling in and are happy with the work we are giving you?" Dominic was trying to make Emma feel comfortable and more relaxed as he could see she was nervous.

"Definitely," she stressed emphatically. "I'm determined to prove to you and Charles that by appointing me, you both made the right decision. I promise I won't let you down."

"I have every faith in you as I can already see that you have a strong work ethic," he replied encouragingly.

By this time, they had made their way out of the city. As it was nearing lunch time, the traffic seemed to be getting busier. Fortunately, they were driving in the opposite direction to the main body of vehicles and their overpowering exhaust fumes. They were heading north of the city to a suburb called Finchley, just over eight miles away from the gallery. "It shouldn't take us long to get there provided there aren't any traffic jams." Dominic explained to her whilst he was concentrating on the road. "Do you know this part of London?" He asked genuinely.

"Not really. Although I live in Ruislip, at the moment, which isn't a million miles away, I have never had any reason to go anywhere else except to the city or the West End." She felt this made her sound so lame and unadventurous, like she was a tourist, content not to stray from the stereotype areas stated in their guides. She wished she'd kept quiet and looked over at Dominic to see his reaction but thankfully he was smiling.

As they reached Finchley, he began explaining the reason for their ride out and the possible new client they were going to meet. Even though he had hinted about it earlier, she was still eager to listen to the brief. They would be visiting a gentleman, a Mr Bloom, who was born in Austria and had in his possession a Klimt sketch that was apparently given to him by his father. "It sounds very promising," Dominic stated hopefully, "but until we are able to study it fully, we mustn't get too excited." Emma couldn't help but show her excitement as this would definitely be a first for her to be at the forefront of a new acquisition and of such a prestigious artist. She was already favouring a sketch that the gallery had of another work by him, which soon they would be able to compare it with.

Mr Viktor Bloom opened the door of his detached 1930s property which was situated in a secluded, up-market, residential area of Finchley and welcomed them inside.

"Good morning, Mr Bloom. I am Dominic Hadley and this is my assistant, Emma, who has recently joined our team at The Hadley Gallery as a trainee evaluator. We are very pleased you chose us to oversee the authentication of the property in question." Dominic said authoritatively.

"Come in, come in, please," he said excitedly. "I've been looking forward to our meeting." He ushered them into a fairly large room with an oval mahogany table surrounded by ten chairs at its centre. There were piles of books and catalogues stacked at one end which brought to Emma's mind her cluttered office, but there the similarity ended. Heavy dark red brocade curtains were draped at the windows and also at the French doors that led into the garden beyond; which gave the appearance of being in a grand theatre waiting for the opera to begin. She could see that the furnishings had been elegant once, probably about thirty years ago; but now outdated although the style suited the room along with the crystal chandelier that was suspended from an ornate, plaster-carved ceiling rose.

"Would you like a cup of tea before we start?" Mr Bloom asked kindly. We had rushed out of the gallery earlier and only then realised we were both quite thirsty and that wouldn't be conducive towards serious discussions with us croaking due to our dry throats.

"That would be most appreciated, thank you." Dominic replied for us both. Mr Bloom, still standing by the door, called out instructions to an empty hallway and unbelievably, within ten minutes we were sitting, sipping lemon tea from glass beakers. His housekeeper of four years, since his wife died, had brought the tray in for us. Also arranged on the tray was a plate of apple strudel slices from a cake she had only made that morning.

"Hannah's a wonderful cook, her strudel is the best in Finchley so enjoy, please!" he said convincingly. I didn't hesitate, after all, it would be rude not to, I thought. Dominic looked at me questioningly and I realised I wasn't being very professional and quickly devoured the cake while suppressing the urge to gulp.

Dominic wanted to know the history relating to the provenance of the sketch. "Mr Bloom, are you able to elucidate the reason for us being here; do you ultimately wish to sell it to the gallery, whatever the outcome?" he asked bluntly.

Slightly taken aback by Dominic's forthrightness, Mr Bloom proceeded to relate to us the history behind his beautiful sketch.

"I was born in Vienna, Austria in 1910 into a loving Jewish family. Before my father, Berret, had met and married my mother, he had worked for an engraver called Ernst who also happened to be Gustav Klimt's brother. The three of them in 1883, the brothers Gustav and Ernst and my father Berret had shared the same studio alongside Franz, a close friend of the Klimt brothers; this was before Klimt had become really famous. By 1890, they were then becoming known in Vienna as a conservative art group and in 1891, Gustav Klimt first asked Ernst's sister-in-law to model for him. Her name was Emilie, and she is present in many of his paintings. She was so beautiful in a typically, bohemian way with naturally wavy, auburn red hair flowing onto to her shoulders that my father fell immediately and hopelessly in love with her. He would try to be present each time she came to sit for Gustav in the hope she would return his affections but to no avail.

He even tried to cajole the artist to use him as the male model so that he would be close to her and imagine they were the true lovers depicted in the painting. Klimt just laughed and told him if he grew another ten inches, he might then consider it. Being only five foot three inches, my father was not the epitome of male perfection and although it hurt him being told this, deep down, he realised it was true. So, Klimt promised to give his good friend a gift in 1907 of one of the few sketches he had made of the 'loving couple' as a consolation. Klimt didn't seem to value his sketches then. There was even a rumour that he allowed his pet cats to play and scratch them to shreds, but even so, my father cherished that sketch as proof of their close friendship. My father soon overcame his unrequited love for Emilie and went on to marry my mother.

They had three children, myself being the youngest; probably, more an afterthought or even an accident but loved all the same. The atmosphere in Vienna was becoming uncomfortable, to put it mildly, if you were a Jewish family, and so, my father made the decision that we should leave and changed our name from Blomstein to Bloom. We settled in Paris for five years until yet again anti-Semitism raised its ugly head and so once more, we had to up sticks. Thankfully, England welcomed us and we were able to begin to relax and build a good, secure life once more. Sadly, I am the sole survivor as my siblings died several years ago and unfortunately, my wife and I were never blessed with any children. So, inevitably the Klimt sketch is now in my possession." With rheumy eyes beginning to form tears, Mr Bloom forced himself back out of the past and into the room reluctantly.

"What an enthralling story and thank you so much for sharing that glimpse of your family's life with us." Dominic said with genuine feeling. "We would now appreciate it if you could show us the actual art work in question, and I trust that you have it here in your house and not secreted away in a bank vault somewhere." This was Dominic's flimsy attempt at being official as Emma could see Mr Bloom's brief depiction of his Austrian roots had touched him.

Victor Bloom pushed himself, with an effort, out of the red upholstered dining chair he had been sitting in and proceeded towards the door. "Would you like to follow me, please?" He said resignedly. "My beloved sketch is hanging in my bedroom upstairs."

We proceeded slowly behind him, taking each stair as if we were ascending a steep hill; one step cautiously at a time in pace with the eighty-nine-year-old Mr Bloom's slow progress. The staircase wound round to the right with several doors visibly leading from it. We followed him down to the last door at the end of the hall which he stated was his bedroom. As he opened the door, a waft of stale, dusty air greeted us. It was dark inside, as the curtains had not been opened, so at first it was hard to see too much but our eyes soon adjusted to the dimness.

"I'm sorry, I should have told you that I keep the sketch hidden in this darkened room as I don't sleep in here anymore," Mr Bloom explained apologetically. "I don't have the strength to climb the stairs every night; instead, I have a small but sufficient room downstairs for me to lay my old head."

"It was wise that the sketch had been kept without direct sunlight on it, otherwise it would have deteriorated." Dominic added as he handed me a small torchlight. "Okay, Emma, I want you to point the light at it so that we can get to see it better."

"Goodness, it's magnificent." Emma said holding her breath as the full beauty of the sketch became visible. "It's absolutely wonderful." Other superlatives came to mind but nothing else was needed as it spoke for itself. An illusion of familiarity swept over her as she shone the beam of the torchlight directly onto the faces of the perfectly sketched embracing couple; like an unexplainable feeling of déjà vu.

"We will need to take it with us to the gallery to study it closely, if that is all right with you, Mr Bloom?" Dominic asked, while frowning at Emma's glazed expression and jolting her back into the present. "We must be going now," he added looking at her to agree with him.

"Please, call me Viktor now as I feel that I can trust you both with my precious heirloom." With that, he asked Dominic to unhook the sketch from the wall and to bring it downstairs where there was a roll of bubble-wrap, brown paper and string waiting to be used. The Klimt sketch carefully wrapped, we thanked Viktor for his hospitality and promised we would be treating his prized possession with the utmost care.

"I just need you to sign this document before we leave," Dominic said as he retrieved an envelope from his briefcase and handed it to Mr Bloom. "It is to verify that you have willingly given The Hadley Gallery in Covent Garden full permission to remove from your premises, for a short period, the sketch of 'The Kiss' by Gustav Klimt for authentication and valuation purposes only. It will be included in our insurance while it is in our custody. I hope this is agreeable to you?" Dominic stated. Viktor Bloom had anticipated this and had his Parker fountain pen at hand, which had been a present to him from his wife on his sixtieth birthday and had only been used twice before. Once signed, he handed the document back to Dominic.

"I look forward to hearing from you soon, please God, hopefully with good news." He called out as he was waving goodbye to us. He watched us place the art work carefully in the boot of the Mercedes and waited for us to leave before he closed his door, like we were his children going off to school.

"That was the most amazing experience," I blurted out as soon as I sat in the passenger seat. "What a lovely, kind man. I just hope that what we were told was all true and it turns out to be genuine." *I'm sure it was*, I thought to myself.

Chapter Four

Dominic insisted that we needed to have some lunch before heading back to the gallery. He was hungry, so he felt sure I would be.

"I know a little Turkish restaurant not far from The Hadley, very informal but lovely authentic cuisine. Do you like Turkish food, Emma?" He asked hopefully.

"I agree, I would like something to eat, but I've never had Turkish food before. Is it spicy as I'm not too keen on hot, spicy food?" She said feeling pathetic. "And don't you think we should be heading straight back to work, after all, I don't want to get into trouble with the boss for being late?" Emma said with a mischievous smile.

"This boss has suggested it, so just relax; we have had a busy morning, and are in need of some sustenance now." He replied with a wink.

The Sarastro restaurant in Drury Lane was a popular haunt for theatre goers and opera lovers. It was not far from Covent Garden, within walking distance if need be. There was enough room outside on the pavement for a few café-style tables and chairs; set ready with white table cloths on which were placed smaller, red square ones, lightly flapping in the slight breeze, like an array of bunting. Dominic, however, guided Emma towards a table for two inside the restaurant, near the window where it was lighter and less intimate. He didn't want her to misconstrue this as anything more than a business lunch, although he did feel a slight thrill surge through him momentarily. He imagined briefly the image that they would be perceived as: professional, smart, young middle-aged business man with attractive, much younger woman, an obvious conclusion would be they're having an affair. He wasn't sure whether he secretly wished it to be true.

Emma must have honed in on Dominic's feelings at that moment as she admonished herself for having similar thoughts. Sensing this, she felt hot and knew her face was turning a lovely shade of crimson, so she quickly excused herself and dashed off to the ladies' room. When she returned, after five minutes of splashing water on her face to cool it down, the waiter had already taken Dominic's order.

"I hope you don't mind but I've taken the initiative and ordered a meze for us both to share. I'm sure you'll like it as this is a selection of mild dishes. I've also ordered a glass of wine each to celebrate today's acquisition." He knew this was being a bit premature but he was in a good mood and glad to be sharing it with even better company. It was already after 2 pm when they began eating, so it was unusually empty as the matinée crowds had already excitedly vacated and were heading towards their pre-booked theatre shows. Emma was enthralled with the internal décor, which portrayed the inside of a theatre with even a balcony where on weekend evenings an opera singer would perform to the delight of the diners. Dominic explained with authority; it was known as 'the show after the show'.

Emma enjoyed the meal but felt self-conscious and tried hard not to splash her clean, white blouse with some of the juices seeping from the food; not a good look having a brown stain appear down the front of your clothes, definitely not the image she wanted to portray, and giggled inwardly.

"Let us toast Viktor Bloom and his sketch." Dominic stated as he raised his glass of wine to meet hers. Emma copied him and realised how relaxed they had become during the meal. He asked her if she would like another glass of wine but she declined as she wanted a clear head for work later. He ordered another glass for himself instead. As he was drinking, his speech became softer and she could see he was loosening up and becoming more like her friend than her boss. "Have you ever been to a casino, Emma? I'll have to take you there one day as there's nothing like seeing that roulette wheel spinning and the anticipation of where it will stop." He said with a faraway look in his eyes. "It certainly boosts the adrenaline." He added draining his wine glass. Emma could see he wasn't really waiting for her to answer his question; it was as if he was reminiscing once of a fortune won.

"I want you to know, Emma, how pleased we are to have you on board and don't hesitate to come to me for guidance. I'll always be there to help you, anytime." He must have realised he had overstepped their professional relationship and covered it up by asking the waiter for the bill. Emma embarrassingly mumbled her thanks and stood up to make him aware that they should be going.

They drove back to The Hadley in silence. Fortunately, it was only a short, ten-minute ride away. Relieved when they arrived, Dominic let Emma jump out of the car while he proceeded to the car park. As she walked into the gallery, Helena was there in front of her, as if she'd been waiting all morning for their return.

"Well, was it a fruitful meeting? Was the journey worthwhile as you've been gone such a long time?" Helena jealously rebuked.

"Yes, I most definitely think so. Why don't you ask Dominic?" As Emma finished saying this, Dominic walked into the gallery holding the brown paper parcel carefully.

"Let us take it down to your office, Emma, as I would like this to be your assignment but obviously with my assistance when required." He said encouragingly.

"Am I allowed to join your party?" Helena said enviously. "I would also like to be included otherwise how do you expect me to make any progress." With that, she gave her uncle the best smile she could muster that effectively reached her beautiful liquid brown eyes and knew he wouldn't be able to resist her request.

"Okay, but just to observe and not to get in our way, you promise?" He added letting her win.

"Of course, whatever you say, *Uncle*." Helena looked triumphantly at Emma as she replied.

The three of them, led by Dominic, descended the stairs to Emma's basement office. It was a bit of a tight squeeze once inside as the room was barely large enough to house one person let alone three.

"I'm sorry, Helena, but I think you'll have to sit this one out as it's too cramped in here even with the door left open." He apologetically smiled at Helena hoping she would understand. "We'll involve you another time once it's been brought up to the main gallery, perhaps." He added.

"Why can't the sketch be brought to your or my father's office instead?" She questioned angrily.

"Because both Charles and I are working on other projects that are also of importance, so please try to understand our predicament and be affable about it. Your time will come soon, I promise." He said firmly, making her aware that the conversation was finished.

She threw a resentful look at Emma before she reluctantly left the office and purposely slammed the door shut. This caused the little window in the corner to rattle and papers to be blown off the desk in the draught. "Oh dear," Emma thought to herself, *I think I'll have to watch my back with her, she's going to cause me trouble one day.* The instinct she had felt when she had first been told about Helena was now more than just a hunch, it was now being validated.

"I'm so sorry, Emma, that you had to witness such a childish display. Helena is still young and needs to control her moods but that will come with experience, so please don't judge her too harshly." He said trying to smooth over the previous awkward situation whilst collecting the papers that had been blown onto the floor. "Now, let us forget about that and unwrap this delightful package." Regaining his professional stature, he proceeded to cut the string which had been holding the paper securely.

Dominic eased the paper and the bubble-wrap carefully away to reveal the sketch in all its glory. At that moment, the sun's rays had managed to penetrate through the grimy office window to magically illuminate it further causing Emma to gasp and catch her breath. And now they could see it in a brighter light; it was magnificent, a wonderful piece of art. Instantly, it captured Emma's heart and imagination as she recalled Mr Bloom's romantic story of its provenance.

"I think I'm in love." Emma blurted out realising that never before had a work of art affected her so much and how immature she must have sounded. Dominic just laughed as he knew the effect of seeing and holding such a beautiful piece of art, so closely, can have on an impressionable person like Emma. In fact, it pleased him to see her being so conscientious and enthralled in her work.

They remained together for the rest of the afternoon studying the decisive strokes of both watercolour and pencil on the antique parchment; capturing Klimt's genius for immortalising his subject. With their bodies in close proximity and their heads nearly touching each other, Emma was beginning to succumb to the Klimt magic that seemed to be emanating from this beautiful drawing. They both felt the frisson between them but weren't sure whether to act on it. She wanted him to kiss her and instinctively knew he shouldn't. *Why not,* she thought to herself. "I'm unattached and I think so is he. Go for it then," said a risqué voice inside her head urging her on. They both looked up in unison as if they were reading each other's minds. As their lips were about to meet, a noise on the stairs outside the room alerted them. Immediately, they sprang apart as Helena pushed open the door that had been left slightly ajar.

Unsure of whether his niece had witnessed anything, Dominic momentarily froze and then blustering, stated it was getting late and he needed to go as he had another meeting that evening. Before he left, he ordered Emma, in an authoritative voice, to take images of the sketch at every angle and then to wrap it back up and to place it in the company's safe for the night. He rattled out the safe's combination for her to take note of which she quickly wrote down on a scrap of paper and then he hurriedly left the office.

Helena seething with jealousy just stood still, staring at Emma. Yes, she had seen what was about to happen between them and was glad she had prevented it.

Following Dominic's example, Emma said she also needed to leave as she was meeting a friend for late night shopping at the Brent Cross Shopping Centre at 6.30 pm. She didn't want to get into a confrontation with Helena, so she quickly wrapped the sketch, grabbed the paper with the safe numbers on and rushed up to Charles' office where the safe was housed in the far corner of the room. Thankfully, Charles had already left for the day, so she was saved from having to have a conversation with him which, in the circumstances, she could have done without. Meticulously, she punched the combination into the safe, waited to hear the click and then pulled the strong, metal door open. She whispered goodnight to the sketch as she placed it carefully inside, likening it to tucking up a baby in its cot, then shut the door firmly and turned the handle so that it was secure. She breathed a sigh of relief thanking inwardly for the day's end and what an eventful day it had been. With mixed emotions about all that had occurred, she hurried to meet her friend. Only remembering too late, once she was sitting on the tube carrying her towards Brent Cross, that she had left the scrap of paper on which she had hurriedly jotted down the combination numbers, on Charles' desk. *Still, I'm sure it'll be safe there until the morning.*

Chapter Five

The cleaners had just arrived as Emma was rushing out of the gallery; she held the door open for them as they struggled with their equipment to enter the premises. "Goodnight, I hope you won't find my office too messy." She called out over her shoulder as she hurried off into the dusk; the clocks hadn't gone back yet for winter, but in a couple of weeks it'll be dark by now, she thought as she hurried to the station.

They were a man and wife team; Tony and Shirley Collins, the cleaners who had been cleaning The Hadley offices for several years. They had been recommended to Charles five years ago by an associate of his who had been using their services for a while and found them to be honest, reliable and trustworthy. Usually, they let themselves into the premises as Charles had entrusted them with a set of keys two years ago. It proved a convenient arrangement as it wasn't always possible for Charles or Dominic to be around at that time, which meant the offices were left not cleaned, sometimes for several days. They proceeded towards the rear of the gallery where Dominic's office was the first office to be cleaned. Chatting together whilst tidying and dusting, they were unaware that anyone else was in the building. Usually by 7 pm, no one else was around, unless there was a private viewing in the main gallery in which case, they would have been pre-warned; then the cleaning would be delayed until early the following morning.

Helena, meanwhile, still fuming with Dominic and Emma for excluding her, which she felt they had pre-planned to their own advantage, had followed Emma, unbeknown to her, upstairs to Charles' office. She had watched Emma through the gap in the doorway as she had placed the sketch into the safe. When Emma had rushed out, Helena had hidden herself inside the stationery cupboard which was conveniently placed to the left of the office. She knew also the switch to the security cameras was in there. "Perfect, this'll be easy." She grinned.

Once she knew the coast was clear, Helena emerged quietly from the cupboard and quickly entered Charles' office and closed the door. She thought she had heard the Collins's start cleaning Dominic's office, so she knew she had to hurry up as she didn't want them to know she was still in the building. She had watched Emma read out loud the combination to the safe and then place the scrap of paper, it was written on, onto Charles' desk.

"Here, it is just as I expected," she said feeling pleased with herself. "Now I'm going to make sure she won't be hanging around for much longer. Goodbye, Miss Goody-Goody." She then carefully punched the numbers into the safe's mechanism and pulled the heavy, metal door open; just as Emma had done not thirty minutes previously.

There it was, neatly tied and hers to retrieve. Luckily, Helena had brought to work that day her oversized, tan leather Hermès shoulder bag, so the Klimt sketch slipped into it perfectly. She closed the safe as quietly as she could, screwed up the scrap of paper and threw it into the wastepaper bin and then tiptoed carefully out of the office. She then quickly nipped back into the stationery cupboard and switched the cameras back on. "Brilliant, no-one will know. I think I've found my true vocation as a cat burglar." She laughed *sotto voce*.

Mr and Mrs Collins were still busy in Dominic's office as she could now hear the droning of the vacuum cleaner above the noise of their radio which they regularly played at full blast resonating around the gallery; the pop music seemed incongruous with all the fine art. Helena used this to her advantage to cover any noise she might make herself. Once again, she tiptoed stealthily into the gallery area and then with a spurt on, was out of the front door in a flash.

The thrill of what she had just achieved surged through her whole body. She knew she had committed an offence but it was just a means to an end, she thought to herself. To justify her actions, she decided she will taunt her nemesis further by going to Brent Cross and hopefully catch up with Emma; the perfect alibi.

Chapter Six

Emma had previously arranged to meet her friend Alice in the Costa coffee shop near John Lewis. As it was Friday evening, the centre was busy with nearby office workers, relieved it was the weekend at last and only too eager to spend their hard-earned salaries on themselves. Brent Cross wasn't the largest of shopping centres but nevertheless, it had quite a variety of shops, cafés and wine bars which gave it a bright party atmosphere especially after 6 pm at the end of the working week. It was late night shopping, so it wouldn't be closing until 9 pm, allowing plenty of time to unwind and relax.

She could see Alice sitting at one of the outside café tables, which with some imagination tried to imitate a boulevard in Paris without success, as after all, this was an enclosed shopping centre in north London and not the city of love. It was still preferable to sit outside than being inside a noisy, usually stale, smoky atmosphere.

"Hi, Alice, have you been waiting long?" Emma asked as she could see her friend had already drunk half a glass of her cappuccino before she had arrived. "Sorry, but it was hectic at work today," she added as she was going inside to get herself one of those much-needed refreshments. "Would you like another one?" She called out as an afterthought as she pulled open the café door.

"No thanks," Alice replied. "Perhaps, we can go to a wine bar soon instead? I think my body requires a bit more than just caffeine to revive it." She said hoping Emma will appreciate that idea. Alice had no one to rush home to, not even a parent, as she had left home at nineteen after numerous arguments with them on propriety; they were both devout Presbyterians and stifled her natural free spiritedness. So, often alone in her rented flat, she wished her life then had been different and missed the warmth of a close-knit family.

Sitting drinking their coffees, they proceeded to fill each other in on their respective workloads. Alice bemoaning again the fact that she was still in a dead-end job working as a travel agent in Northolt with no chance of promotion, although she had the advantage of cheap travel which was the only obvious perk. Alice and Emma met at a youth club when they were thirteen and had remained good friends. They were quite opposite in looks; Alice being fairly short and sporting a boyish, blond haircut similar to the one favoured by the then model 'Twiggy' in the sixties, whilst Emma was much taller, slender with shoulder-length, wavy auburn hair. But they shared a love of adventure and both wanted to wring as much as they could from life before they settled into 'normality' as they referred to marriage. Neither of them had a boyfriend at the moment but they weren't too disturbed by this as it gave them the opportunity to re-evaluate their friendship and plan exciting holidays together; last winter, they had booked a skiing weekend in Valloire, France. Even with Alice's discount on travel, it proved too expensive and they had to wait for their next month's pay before they could afford anything more than baked beans to eat. But they both agreed it was worth it just for the après ski experience alone.

Emma had just begun to relate to Alice all that had happened to her that day when she was shocked to see Helena alighting from the nearby escalator. She hadn't had time to get to the juicy part about her and Dominic nearly kissing, when Helena, on seeing Emma, waved and headed in their direction. Before she could warn Alice, Helena was standing in front of them, all smiles as if the previous altercation back at work had been in her imagination.

"Oh, Helena, I didn't realise you were also coming here this evening?" Emma said questioning her sudden appearance.

"I would have told you but you rushed off in such a terrible hurry before I had time to mention it and to grab my bag." Helena replied with her sweetest smile and making a point of adjusting her guilty, leather, Hermès bag to her other shoulder. "Otherwise, we could have travelled here together. Never mind, aren't you going to introduce me to your friend?"

Emma couldn't believe the audacity of this sly, mischievous, young girl pretending to be friendly and wondered what the reason was behind this sudden show of affability. She choked out their introductions, hoping Alice would realise by her own demeanour, not to be deceived by the false impression of the sweet, warm colleague Helena was trying to portray.

"We were about to go up to the wine bar on the top floor, if you would like to join us?" Emma felt compelled to ask her but secretly hoped she would decline the invitation.

"Thank you, but I won't if that's okay? I need to collect a gift I'd ordered from John Lewis for my parents' anniversary next week. I appreciate you including me though." With that, Helena said goodbye and headed towards the store situated at the end of the shopping centre.

"My goodness!" Emma exclaimed. "I can't believe she had the cheek to befriend me as if we're the best of colleagues. I'm sure she hates my guts and I'm usually right about these things. She's up to something, I feel positive about that." She said worriedly.

"Give her a chance, she seemed okay to me, perhaps she's not as bad as you're implying. After all, she's only young and obviously out to impress with her smart, designer holdall she ostentatiously kept moving from shoulder to shoulder." As if we could have missed that, Emma wanted to add but didn't want to sound catty.

They drank the remains of their coffees and headed straight to the nearest wine bar, hoping they wouldn't bump into Helena again. Once they were settled on a comfy, imitation velvet banquette with their extravagantly, colourful cocktails containing everything but the obligatory paper umbrella, Emma proceeded to embellish to Alice, her near romantic liaison with Dominic. Wishing the kiss had actually happened. "Bloody, Helena!" she swore to herself.

Chapter Seven

As it was Saturday morning, Emma gave herself an extra hour in bed. The gallery opened late at the weekend; at 10.30 am instead of 9.30 am as on weekdays. She only had one in four Saturdays off, today wasn't that one, but she didn't mind as yesterday had been so eventful. As she lay reminiscing of her and Dominic's closeness, she felt a warm glow gradually spread from her toes to her neck, making her fling open the duvet as she suddenly felt too hot; literally and mentally. She hoped he would be at work today but couldn't remember if he said he would be seeing any clients in the gallery for initial viewings. Perhaps, they'll be working the whole day alone without anyone else there to distract them, she fantasised, as she was cleaning her teeth and gazing dreamily into the bathroom mirror.

"Now, what shall I wear," she said out loud to herself as she opened the sliding mirrored door to her wardrobe. "I know something attractive and feminine; demure but statement making at the same time." She decided on a striped, silk, mid-length shirt dress in autumnal shades and cinched in at the waist with an amber coloured patent leather belt; practical for work but clings in all the right places for effect. She then pulled out from the bottom of her wardrobe a pair of tan leather ankle boots with three-inch heel, to complete the outfit. *Perfect.* "My feet might ache by the end of the day but a girl has to suffer if it gets her noticed." She said to herself convincingly. She could see the morning was bright, as a ray of sunlight bounced through the hall side-window leaving dust motes dancing in the air. She grabbed her jacket off the coat stand where she had hung it the previous evening and opened the street door.

"Bye, Mum, I'm in a rush, see you tonight." She called out guiltily, knowing that lately she hadn't been there much for the special mother and daughter chats she knew her mum savoured. "Perhaps, this evening I'll spend time with her to make up for it," she said to herself as she was walking to the station.

Travelling on the underground to work, she knew she had achieved the look she had aimed for as she received several admiring glances from some of the male passengers sitting opposite her on the tube as they peered surreptitiously around their newspapers they were pretending to read. Feeling confident, she alighted at Covent Garden station and rode up in the lift to the street. Normally, in the week, it was crowded with much pushing and shoving and treading on toes to get into the lift, like being packed into a cage. Fortunately, today it was the opposite and she didn't have to contend with people's elbows or feet touching any part of her anatomy. The Hadley was only a short walk away in the bustling, vibrant street of Long Acre, so hopefully, she'll manage the distance without tripping up in her high-heeled boots. That would definitely not be a good look and smiled inwardly imagining the scene.

As soon as she entered the gallery, she knew something was amiss. All thoughts of a possible blossoming romance happening between her and Dominic flew swiftly from her mind like pheasants hearing a gunshot during the 'open season'.

Both Dominic and Charles were standing in the main gallery with worried looks on their faces. *Charles didn't usually come into work on a Saturday,* she thought to herself, *so Dominic must have called him in.* It must be serious. They had obviously been waiting for her to arrive.

"Hello, Emma, would you please come into my office." Charles said in a grim voice. She followed him into his office with Dominic close behind her. "Take a seat, please." Charles said offering her a chair and placing it adjacent to his desk. This was reminiscent of her interview, *so perhaps I'm getting the sack* she thought nervously to herself and crossed her fingers hoping this wasn't the case. Dominic joined his brother as they stood together in front of her.

"I need you to tell me verbatim your movements before you left the gallery last night as both Dominic and I had already gone by then." Charles said, and threw Dominic an angry look for not being around to supervise the closing procedure of the previous day.

Gosh, it must be serious if Charles is quoting Latin at me, Emma thought before she proceeded to recall her exact movements, on Charles' insistence, for them both. It made her feel as if she was on trial in a witness box with two judges and no jury.

"Can I ask why you need to interrogate me, what has happened?" Emma questioned and began to feel angry at her mistreatment.

Dominic proceeded to explain that he had arrived early, before the gallery had opened, so that he could have another good look at the Klimt sketch before any clients arrived. He opened the safe and expected to see the sketch inside but, to his amazement, it wasn't there. He then thought, perhaps Emma had left it on her desk in error having not remembered the combination numbers; but he knew she had quickly written them down on a piece of paper. Worried, he called Charles and together they searched the entire premises together in case it had been misplaced.

"That is the reason we need to know where you put it and whether you were the last person to see it before leaving the gallery?" He asked, hoping that she will be able to solve the mystery.

Emma began trembling with shock at this revelation and she was aware of tears beginning to run down her cheeks; which only an hour ago had been plumped up from permanently smiling. It was hard to comprehend how life can change so dramatically, she thought.

"I definitely placed it carefully inside the safe. I even made sure the door had shut firmly and I heard the click to verify this." Emma said trying to sound positive. "The only people left on the premises were the cleaners, they had just arrived as I was leaving, in fact, I held the door open for them as they struggled in with their equipment." She added picturing the scene in her mind.

"So, no one else could have had access to the safe?" Charles asked questioningly.

"No, I don't think so," she said unconvincingly. "In my rush to go home, I did leave Helena in my office but she must have left quite soon after me as I saw her at Brent Cross shopping centre not long after I had arrived there. She made a point of saying hello to me and my friend, Alice."

"So, just to confirm what has been said, the Collins couple were the only ones left on the premises, then." Charles reiterated.

"I've just remembered something but I'm afraid to tell you," Emma said hesitantly feeling the tears starting to well up again. "What is that?" he said abruptly. "Please continue."

"Well, in my hurry to meet my friend, I inadvertently forgot to pick up the paper with the combination safe numbers on. I left it on your desk where I had placed it when I opened the safe. It wasn't until I was travelling on the tube that I remembered. I'm so sorry, I thought it would be safe in your office until I could retrieve it today."

"Therefore, it should still be here on my desk, shouldn't it Emma? So where is it now?" Charles said seething with anger and about to burst a blood vessel.

Unable to restrain her emotions any longer, Emma began sobbing openly; hot tears coursing down her beautifully made-up face, leaving streaks of black mascara track marks that joined to form an overflow which then dripped off her chin and onto her silk dress.

And to add insult to injury, neither one of the two men watching her came to comfort her.

Chapter Eight

The gallery remained closed for the rest of the day and all potential clients were cancelled; a huge loss as Saturdays were their 'bunce' days, unexpected sales from browsing weekenders purchasing on a whim, which made a substantial difference to the week's takings. Emma stayed in her office in the basement out of sight, and she felt where she deserved to be; constantly turning over in her mind her exact movements that culminated into this catastrophe. Dominic had brought a mug of tea down to calm her but the only warmth came from the hot drink, there were no words of consolation to help ease her anguish. And the thought of informing Mr Bloom of the misplacement or perhaps theft of his beloved sketch was enough to start her crying again. "No, I must pull myself together and try to solve this enigma." She said speaking out loud and urging herself to be strong and positive.

Meanwhile, upstairs in Charles' office, Tony and Shirley Collins, the two cleaners, had arrived. Charles had called them that morning to ask if they would mind coming in as there had been a serious incident which needed urgent action. He didn't want to say too much over the phone in case they felt they were being accused. They confirmed to Charles that they hadn't seen anyone else in the building after Emma had left. But they couldn't swear to it as what with the vacuum cleaner being on most of the time, they wouldn't have heard anything else; or as Tony described, "World War III could have started and we'd be oblivious."

Charles also asked them if they had seen a piece of paper on his desk with random numbers scribbled on it but being careful not to intimate the importance of the said paper. In reply to this, they both denied, indignantly, seeing anything of relevance on any of the desks that would be of interest to them; whether it be numerals or anything else for that matter. They just do the job they've always done; clean, dust, vacuum and empty wastepaper bins, as the contract itemised when they first started cleaning for The Hadley.

"Aren't you happy with our services, then?" Tony Collins indignantly asked Charles. "Or are we being accused of something?"

"Of course not, it's just we have found ourselves in a predicament and need to know everyone's whereabouts of yesterday evening." Charles replied trying to placate Tony who he could see was beginning to get agitated. "Something you said has sparked a modicum of interest, though. You mentioned emptying the bins. What do you empty them into and then where do you take it?" Charles asked hopefully.

"That's easy, we put all the rubbish from the bins into a black refuse sack which we then place inside your industrial wheelie bin outside in the back alleyway." Tony replied perplexed by all these questions.

Charles asked Tony to follow him to retrieve the offending black sack. He knew it must be on the top of the bin as nothing else had been emptied or thrown into it since. He untied the knot and emptied the rubbish onto the courtyard. After sifting through clumps of dust, pungent, blackened banana skins, brown apple cores and other detritus, Charles found what he had been searching for; a screwed-up piece of paper with the offending numerals scribbled on it.

"Eureka!" Charles shouted out. He knew this proved the Collins couple were innocent and could be exonerated from the crime in question. After all, they wouldn't have known the relevance of the paper if it had already been screwed up inside the bin when they emptied it. Although, it still remained a mystery as to who could have thrown the paper there in the first place.

Charles thanked Tony and Shirley Collins for their assistance in this matter and apologised profusely to them as he was showing them out of the gallery; stressing also the value of their work to the company. He hoped this would appease them for any discomfort they might have felt.

"We are still no nearer to finding the sketch." Charles stated, looking to Dominic for some guidance as to where they should now pursue. "Perhaps, it's time now for contacting the police." Dominic replied reluctantly. "I know it's the last resort, but unless something else comes to light, we must treat this as a theft of a very expensive piece of property that was in our care." He sighed and the blood drained from his face as he was imagining the inevitable conversation, he would soon be having with dear Mr Bloom.

"Were you able to check the CCTV cameras in my office and around the gallery before I arrived this morning?" Charles asked Dominic, assuming he would confirm that he had. "Yes, it was the first thing I did after calling you, but

I didn't spot anything unusual; just the normal activity of the day with Helena, Emma and then the cleaners when they arrived." He confirmed. "There *was* a slight discrepancy, come to think about it, the cameras did blank out momentarily but only for five minutes, I assumed it must have been a power cut. Or so I thought." He added worriedly.

Chapter Nine

As Helena opened her eyes the next morning, it all came flooding back to her. "I'm a thief now, there's no denying it. Oh God! What have I done?" she said out loud. "I'll go to prison and get a criminal record. What was I thinking of; I only wanted to teach her a lesson, it seemed like a good idea at the time?" She knew instinctively she had gone too far this time but *what's done is done*, she thought, *so now I've just got to make the best of it and not get discovered.*

She was used to 'taking' things but most of the time they belonged to her family; so, she justified that as borrowing and not stealing. *Obviously, no one noticed any of their trinkets missing or I would have heard about it and anyway, they can afford it, she thought. Last week, I 'borrowed' Mum's pink, pearl earrings without asking her as I knew she would refuse me but they went so well with my new cream and pink, silk, leopard print Givenchy jump suit I wore to Samantha's party last Saturday. Shame, I lost one though, it must have been in her garden when I was snogging that creep, Alex. "Ugh!"* she recoiled at that thought and definitely decided she shouldn't drink so many Pimms.

As it was Saturday morning, she knew her mother, Sadie, would already be at the hairdressers in Sloane Square where she went every week without fail to have her blond hair immaculately blow-dried or once every six weeks for her highlights to be enhanced. Her father, Charles, sometimes drove her there so that he could spend some time on his own shopping in Peter Jones, if it was something for the house or any bespoke gentleman establishment if he required new attire for himself. Either way, she knew she was on her own.

She saw her Hermès bag in the corner of her room where she had flung it the night before. She opened it gingerly, hoping she hadn't damaged it; after all, it might be worth a pretty penny. There it was, still intact as before, wrapped up in its brown paper and string. Thinking of all the designer clothes she would be able to acquire from selling it, she said out loud in excitement "That'll be my mission today to go on a shopping spree with my ill-gotten gains." She decided she needed to get rid of it as soon as possible. With an adrenaline rush pumping through her at the thought of all she could buy, she pulled on a pair of blue, stone-washed jeans that had been lying amongst other discarded clothing she had left in a pile on her bedroom floor; how often her mother had remonstrated with her to tidy everything up *but what's the point if you're only going to put them on again*? Thinking that, she also found her favourite pale blue sweater under the said pile, now quite creased, *never mind, they'll soon smooth out from the warmth of my body,* she thought to herself.

Grabbing her denim jacket with her large, leather Hermes bag containing the Klimt sketch over one shoulder, she stepped out of her front door and into the early autumn sunlight. Helena lived with her parents in a stylish, bay-windowed detached 1930s house built on a wealthy street in the suburb of Hampstead. Not quite as affluent as Bishop's Avenue but just as snobbish. No one knew or conversed with their neighbours in case they discovered they were wealthier and travelled on more expensive holidays than themselves. As every household owned more than two cars, walking was unheard of and unnecessary, giving more reason to not having to talk to anyone. Helena had been given a brand-new Mini hatchback car in white with pink striping on the roof and wing mirrors, by her parents for her 18th birthday. She had acted surprised when they told her to look outside on the day of her birthday and she saw the car in the driveway, with a huge pink and silver bow with ribbons and balloons attached to it, but she knew deep down, this was the present they were getting her as she had found the receipt from the car dealer in Charles' glove compartment of his silver-grey Bentley. Still, she was thrilled and thanked them profusely as this made it easier for her to show off to her friends and to act superior.

"Now, where would the best place be for me to sell the sketch?" she thought as she was sitting in the driver's seat and adjusting her seat belt. "I can't go to any art dealers or galleries as everyone knows Dad and would wonder why I was selling it and not him." She said to herself. Everyone knows everyone else in the art world unfortunately. "I know, I could pawn it instead, even though I won't get as much money in return, at least it wouldn't be in my possession anymore. After all, I have pawned some of Mum's jewellery before, so hopefully they would accept a piece of art for a change." Feeling pleased with this idea, Helena started the car up and went in search of a pawnbroker.

She knew she had a shopping addiction that was out of control and the only way to feed it was by selling or pawning valuable objects. Her parents were clueless and not aware of her obsession as she didn't always show them her purchases. Plus, she earned a small salary from working at the gallery and they just thought she was being clever and managing her money well. They really didn't know their own child. They thought she was just a privileged young lady enjoying her youth and they encouraged her wholeheartedly; after all, she had worked hard at school and had accomplished becoming head girl. Helena knew this to be her biggest deceit of all, if they but knew it. At the time, she had bribed that year's swat, Jessica who was certainly in line for the title, to a pair of diamond earrings if she would promote Helena as worthy of the headship to their headmistress. So, successfully, yet again she had achieved what she had wanted regardless of any long-term effects. She remembered Sadie being upset at losing her beautiful diamond earrings that had been inherited from her mother; she did feel a pang of remorse seeing her mother so distressed but she knew it would be worth it when they would heap praises on her for becoming head girl and she would bask in their limelight.

Helena remembered a pawnbroker she had used once before in Northolt; that was roughly a year ago, so hopefully she'll be able to keep her anonymity as no one she knew lived in this neck of the woods. She parked her Mini in the nearby multi-storey car park and walked the two hundred or so yards to the high street where the shop was. Luckily, it wasn't raining but even so, she held the parcel close to her body for protection as she hadn't come this far for it to get damaged. She could see the three brass balls denoting the pawnbroker sign, was only fifty yards ahead and so she speeded up her pace eager to get her reward.

The shop was part jewellers and part pawnbroker and had a glass bay window either side of the entrance doorway, reminiscent of an old-fashioned village shop. In the left-hand window was a display of new jewellery with an array of white and yellow gold wedding rings to the front with a selection of bright sparkling diamond and sapphire engagement rings on a shelf above. Men's and ladies' watches were displayed nearer to the door. In the right-hand window, which Helena was more interested in, were all the second-hand items people had brought in; mainly rings being the detritus of broken marriages. She could see, however, the display of household objects on the side shelves waiting to be claimed and loved again; wall clocks, mantle clocks, China figurines of dogs and horses and stylish ladies with parasols, and yes, even an oil painting. This boosted her morale as she was beginning to feel she had come to the wrong place and with this in mind, she raised her shoulders and pulled open the door.

It was fairly dim inside with dark mahogany wooden vitrines as counters and a brown carpet giving in to holes from foot traffic over the years. An elderly man came forward from behind a heavy dark, green curtain. He had grey, thinning hair and bushy eyebrows over piercing slate blue eyes but with a congenial smile, which made him more approachable. He bolstered Helena's courage with a greeting of, "How may I help you, young lady?" He could see that she was holding a parcel close to her, "What have you got there?" He asked her. She placed the parcel on the counter and proceeded to unwrap it whilst going over the story in her mind.

"A friend has asked me to bring this in to you for assessing its value and would like to pawn it temporarily." She said, hoping she sounded confident. He looked at her quizzically and knew instantly that she was the owner and not a mythical friend. "The amount of times he had heard this from people too embarrassed to own up to hardship." He thought to himself. *Still, it suits me to go along with it after all it keeps my business afloat.* Smiling with this in mind, he uncovered the last of the paper and held the sketch up to an overhead fluorescent lamp to take a better look. He knew nothing about art but could see instantly the quality of this piece; just the parchment alone must be fairly valuable, he thought. Taking it to the rear of the shop, he wanted to check it in a stronger light. He reached for his torch from the shelf above his work desk and examined it thoroughly looking for a signature. He could just make one out vaguely, but he wasn't sure of the artist and it might even be a fake.

So, with this in mind, he came up to Helena and offered her £850. "I expected at least £1000," she replied indignantly. "I'll go up to £900 and that is my best offer to you." He said firmly. She pondered this offer and realised it was better than nothing and at least it won't be in her possession any longer. "Okay, I accept your offer." She said grudgingly. He counted out the bank notes in front of her, as this was her request and handed her a signed chitty with the details of their transaction printed on it; to be redeemed within a month or it will be sold.

Satisfied and relieved with her morning's accomplishment, she stuffed the money into her bag, thanked him and left the shop. She had already decided on a new pair of designer shoes being next on her list of 'must haves', and so with the money itching to be spent, she pointed the car towards the West End and headed for its exclusive shops.

Chapter Ten

A police constable arrived the next morning; being a Sunday, the gallery was normally closed to the public unless they were holding a special event. Charles had decided they had no choice but to register the missing sketch as a theft and therefore, a crime which needed to be allocated a number for insurance purposes. Dominic was initially against this as he was hoping it would be recovered before they pursued this line of action.

After taking notes, the constable seemed satisfied with everything Charles and Dominic had told him surrounding the disappearance. He intimated that it was definitely a mystery, unless someone could have slipped in unnoticed but then surely, the CCTV cameras would have recorded this. With this in mind, he said he needed to speak to the other members of staff who had been present and would call back tomorrow when they would be at work. Charles guided him towards the door and then duly showed him off the premises, not before thanking him for his assistance.

Turning to Dominic, Charles worryingly asked, "When shall we tell Mr Bloom about all this? He has a right to know."

"I know, but let's wait another couple of days in case something materialises and then he might never need to find out." He hopefully replied.

"Okay, if you are sure. I need to go home now as Sadie has decided we should have a barbecue in the garden this afternoon due to the Indian summer weather we are experiencing." As an afterthought he said, "Perhaps you would like to come but please don't mention anything to Sadie about all this. I do *not* want her to worry."

"Thank you, I won't, I promise," he replied.

Dominic arrived later that afternoon through a gate leading from the driveway and into the garden, bypassing the need to ring the front doorbell. Charles was busy on the patio, lighting the gas barbecue and arranging all the utensils, ready for using. Playing at being a chef and dressed in a long, blue and white striped apron gave Charles a chance to relax and enjoy being at home with his family. Sadie, meanwhile, was in the kitchen preparing the salads which were to accompany the pre-marinated lamb and chicken fillets, as well as beefburgers and sausages for those who insisted on having them; which would probably be Helena when she decided to get up out of her bed.

Handing Charles a bottle of Pinot Noir, Dominic said, "I hope this meets with your approval, I couldn't come empty handed." Charles nodded in agreement and added it to the other wines and soft drinks on display. "Will Helena be joining us today?" Dominic enquired.

"I expect so eventually. She was out till late last night, so she is still in bed but should be up soon," he replied.

"The police will want to talk to her tomorrow so make sure she has a clear head when she arrives and preferably having an early night will help," Dominic said firmly.

Just then Sadie came out from the house and into the garden, carrying a tray laden with side dishes of salads and placed them on the garden table that was already dressed with cutlery and condiments atop a clean white cloth. Dominic helped her to bring out the meats and bread rolls while she carried out the plates. Charles, delighting in his role as a chef, proceeded to cook the food and to throw a selection of herbs onto the meat which produced a wonderful, appetising aroma.

Helena appeared five minutes later after having smelt a whiff of the food wafting through her open bedroom window. "I'm starving, is it ready?" She demanded. "Sorry, if I look a mess, I'll change later." She added realising she had thrown on an old track suit that needed washing and hadn't brushed her hair yet, or her teeth for that matter. "I wasn't aware Uncle Dominic was going to be here today?" She yawned, still feeling the aftermath of the night before.

"He doesn't have to ask you for permission to visit us, does he?" Charles replied jokingly wanting to sustain the pleasant atmosphere of their informal family get together. "It's a beautiful afternoon with delicious food, cooked perfectly by yours truly," he added bowing. "Now let's eat." Holding the tongs firmly, he lifted the hot pieces of cooked meat onto each of the plates and suggested they should help themselves to the cold buffet that Sadie had laid out for them earlier.

Dominic carried his plate towards a rustic wooden table and chair set that had been strategically placed in the shade of a large fig tree. It was a wide garden rather than long and had been recently landscaped as neither Charles nor Sadie claimed to be gardeners. In one corner was a reasonably sized pond containing a few goldfish but not large enough to house carp, which Charles had originally desired. An established apple tree stood in the opposite corner and gave an abundant crop of cooking apples most years; Sadie was renowned for her pies and crumbles, one of which was on the menu today for dessert accompanied by whipped cream.

After selecting her food, Helena looked around the garden and saw Dominic sitting by himself under the fig tree. She dreamily made her way into his direction and sat down on a chair beside him. "You don't mind if I sit next to you, do you?" She asked tongue in cheek. "You *are* my favourite uncle after all."

"I'm your *only* uncle, so stop this charade and tell me what you've done with the sketch."

"I did as you asked, except I pawned it instead, as selling it would have been too risky." She stated and then recapped him with her expedition to Northolt the previous day and all it entailed.

"Good girl, well done." He praised after she had finished speaking. "We'll leave it there for now until the heat has cooled down before collecting it in a couple of weeks. What have you done with the money by the way?" He questioned, but knowing what her answer was likely to be.

"Already spent on an amazing new pair of boots, I just had to have." She smirked.

"Tomorrow, the police will want to talk to you and Emma at the gallery, so be careful with your answers." He said conspiratorially in a whisper.

"Of course, you haven't got to worry, I'm not stupid." Annoyed at his condescending manner, she got up and walked towards the house leaving her dirty plate on the table for someone else to collect.

Chapter Eleven

It was the start of a new working week and normally, she would be eager to get there; bouncing off the pavement and skipping with energy, like pebbles skimming the sea's surface. Instead, it was the complete opposite, and feeling so dispirited by the recent events, Emma dragged her body listlessly into work.

They were all there to greet her; like a welcoming committee. She could barely raise a smile, not that anyone encouraged her to do so. Charles asked her into his office where a policeman was already there waiting for her to arrive, with his notepad and pen poised. She had been dreading this. She knew the police would have to be involved eventually as there was so much at stake. Nervously, Emma sat down at Charles' request and the constable began his questions. He seemed too young to be a policeman but he still emanated enough authority to make her feel anxious. Yet again, for his benefit, she recalled exactly, as she remembered it, all that had occurred last Friday evening.

She was desperate for a cup of coffee after her traumatic interview as she'd never had any dealings with the police before and her throat was parched. Charles told her to go down to her office and to continue to work as she would normally. The policeman was due to leave once he had Helena's statement but they were still waiting for her to arrive. Emma felt so uneasy, as knowing Helena for the conniving, spoilt little madam she was, she could easily fabricate a scenario which could implicate Emma further.

Trying to push this feeling from her mind, Emma opened the catalogue she had been using to discover as much about Klimt as possible. She tried to concentrate but the thought of that beautiful sketch she had been holding only three days before caused the tears to well in her eyes. "I owe it to that lovely, kind and trusting Mr Bloom to find his heirloom, but how?"

Dominic appeared in her doorway as she was desperately trying to collect her emotions and to calm down. He could see she was distressed by the rogue tear escaping down her cheek. He did feel sorry for her and was genuinely attracted to her, so he came close and put his arm around her for comfort. The warmth of his touch was enough for Emma to cling to his arm for the protection she yearned for. He began stroking her hair to soothe her further, hoping she wouldn't object. But this was exactly what she did want and had been fantasising about. She also needed him to know that she was innocent and that she had been 'set up' but not sure yet, how or by whom. She openly voiced these reservations to him but he just shushed her and continued to stroke her hair to placate her.

He held her hands and pulled her to her feet so that she was standing closely in front of him. She allowed him to enwrap her with his arms and to hold her tightly against his body; so close she could feel his breath on her neck. He tilted her chin so that she was looking directly into his large, brown eyes and hoped that this time she wouldn't be disappointed; she wasn't. He bent his head forward so that their lips were at first tentatively touching and then he held the back of her head firmly making it impossible for her to move and kissed her fully and ardently; a fleeting glimpse of Klimt's lovers entered her thoughts. With her heart beating furiously, she passionately returned his kisses and melted in his arms; all thoughts of any wrongdoings having been erased from her mind.

They guiltily sprang apart as they heard Helena's raised voice shouting indignantly from above. Obviously, she was being interviewed by the young policeman in her father's office. All they could ascertain was Helena's refusal to be interrogated as she had nothing to do with any missing artwork. Dominic raised his perfectly manicured, dark eyebrows in disgust at hearing her behaviour and then caringly asked Emma if she would like to meet him after work for a drink.

Still reeling from their wonderfully illicit embrace, Emma readily agreed and hoped the rest of the day would pass quickly. She couldn't believe how drastically everything could change. Encouraged by Dominic's attention and faith in her, she began to feel more positive and hopeful that maybe a good result can be found after all.

At 6 pm, Emma closed the catalogue she had been using to research 18th century Dutch landscapes for a client and grabbed her jacket and bag from the back of her chair before hurrying up the stairs. Dominic had been waiting for her and together they exited the gallery. Emma turned her head as they closed the door and out of the corner of her eye, she could see Helena scowling in her direction with a sour look pasted on her face.

Dominic took hold of Emma's hand automatically which gave her a thrill as it seemed so natural. They went to a wine bar nearby where Dominic said he often frequented at the end of a stressful day. "Oh, so it was stressful kissing me then?" Emma asked teasingly.

"Not at all, far from it, I'd like to make a habit of it if I may?" He replied. She blushed profusely at his chutzpah but nodded approvingly at the same time; after they'd had a glass of wine each Dominic suggested whether she would like to join him in a light supper back at his apartment. The wine must have loosened her tongue as she felt unable to speak coherently and just nodded again, like those toy dogs on the back shelf of a car.

It only took them half an hour to reach his flat in St John's Wood as he had been driving as if he was late for an urgent appointment. His apartment was on the top floor, obviously, nothing less than the penthouse for Dominic. It was spacious, modern and minimalistic in its décor; white leather sofas adorned with cushions in black and gold. Beautiful abstract art on some of the walls; *Emma wasn't an expert but they looked to be authentic; could one be a Rothko?* She thought to herself looking in wonder at a large painting above his gleaming, chrome fireplace. The floors were highly polished, soft grey veined tiles made to look like marble, but were in fact, wood. Emma had never seen such opulence and was breath taken.

"Make yourself comfortable while I'll make us a drink." Dominic insisted.

"Your home is magnificent, Dominic." Emma stammered in awe of her surroundings.

"Wait until you see the rest of it." He said with a sparkle in his eye and passing her a glass of champagne. They drank their champagne but never quite got to eating anything as he began kissing her and all thoughts of food flew from her mind. She felt mesmerised as he lifted her up in his strong arms and carried her into his bedroom where he laid her gently onto his immaculate king-sized bed. The fresh aroma of newly laundered sheets hit her senses and she knew then she would be unable to resist this handsome, athletic and extremely desirable man and so she succumbed willingly to the inevitable, even though something warned her not to trust him.

They made love several times during the night as she became so captivated by him that she urgently desired the weight of his body on hers and the hardness of him inside her. She knew he was far more experienced than her the way he controlled and heightened every fibre of her being but she gratefully accepted her role of student and him her master. Exhausted, they finally fell asleep as the first blackbird began the dawn chorus in the gardens below. Emma, at that point, vaguely thought that her mother would be worried as she didn't come home and she knew she should have phoned her; they were her last thoughts before drifting off into a sublime unconsciousness.

They were late for work but Dominic didn't seem to be concerned and unhurriedly, he got dressed in front of Emma without showing any embarrassment at his nakedness. She though, waited for him to go to the kitchen to make the coffee before she jumped out of bed and into the bathroom. Feeling refreshed, she joined him there and hoped there would be a piece of toast to accompany the coffee as she was ravenous.

"I knew you would be hungry, so I have scrambled some eggs to go with the smoked salmon." And he promptly presented her with a plate of the delicious food combination.

"Aren't you having any? Surely, you're hungry as well?" she asked remembering his energetic performance of the previous night.

"I'll grab something on the way into the gallery." He replied dismissively waving his hand as if he was swatting away last night's memory. "Talking of work, I'd be grateful if you don't mention any of this to anyone else." He added and again wielding his arms for effect.

Emma found it hard to believe he was the same passionate person that she had slept with; she had spent the night with Yang and woken up with his alter ego, Yin. "I won't," she replied abruptly, making him aware of his coldness towards her.

"I apologise, if I seem preoccupied but I've been thinking about the missing sketch and feel it's time to inform the owner, Mr Bloom. I don't think we can stall telling him any longer, what do you think?" He asked her, reverting back to being her officious, professional boss.

Emma sighed, knowing that any further feelings of love or affection towards this man had to be shelved or she could drastically get hurt.

Chapter Twelve

A week after discovering the sketch had gone missing, Emma once again, accompanied Dominic in his car to Finchley to inform Mr Bloom of the theft of his beautiful sketch. They needed to tell him face to face and as much as Emma was dreading it, a phone call would have been out of the question; the coward's way out. They sat in almost complete silence most of the way there, both imagining the scenario which was about to confront them.

Hannah, Mr Bloom's loyal housekeeper answered their knock and was surprised to see them as she was usually informed in advance of any visitors that were due. Nevertheless, she swiftly showed them into the large dining room they had first entered on their previous visit. After waiting ten minutes, which to Emma felt like an eternity, Mr Bloom entered the room. He looked puzzled to see them again so soon, especially as he hadn't received a progress report concerning the evaluation.

"Please, sit down," Mr Bloom said gesturing towards the dining chairs surrounding the table. "Is there a problem I should know about?" He added after seeing their worried looks and reluctant lack of eye contact towards him.

Dominic then proceeded hesitantly to inform him of the mysterious disappearance of his beloved Klimt sketch. After he had finished explaining in full, the blood seemed to drain from the elderly man's face; a grey pallor washed over him. He tried to stand but his legs were shaking and they began to buckle under him forcing him to sit back down again. He wanted to say something but choked instead on the spittle forming in his mouth. Unable to stay silent any longer, Emma rushed to his aid, calling his name and rubbing his back hoping to ease his anguish and to stop him choking. She opened the door and called out to Hannah to bring a glass of water, urgently! Sensing something was terribly wrong, Hannah appeared almost immediately and could see the state her charge was in and ran to his side. "What has happened to him?" She cried out angrily. Before either Dominic or Emma could answer her, Mr Bloom started gasping for air and clutching at his chest with his face starting to turn purple. "Call for an ambulance, please, he needs help!" Hannah shouted at them.

Shocked at what was happening, Dominic threw his car keys at Emma and ordered her to quickly unhook the back seat so that it was lying flat. "It will be quicker if we take him to the hospital ourselves. Let's hurry!" He urged and then carefully but firmly picked up the ageing, frail Mr Bloom in his arms as if he was a new born baby and carried him out to his car where he laid him gently on the opened-back seat. There was enough space for Hannah to squeeze in next to him so that she could continue to try to keep him calm, and to loosen any clothing that was inhibiting his breathing; his trouser belt and his neck tie that he always insisted on wearing whether he was going out or not.

"Ring the hospital, Emma, so that they are aware of our arrival." Dominic ordered, as he started the engine and slowly moved forward out of the driveway so as not to jolt the patient. Sitting next to him in the front seat, Emma did as she was told without a word, as she had been shocked into silence and was glad Dominic was taking full control of the terrible situation.

They arrived at the Finchley Memorial Hospital, which was less than a mile away, within twenty minutes. Thankfully, the traffic hadn't been against them and Dominic was able to speed up and go over the thirty-mile speed limit hoping he wouldn't get stopped by the police. Mr Bloom and Hannah, who insisted on staying with him, were taken immediately to the emergency room when they arrived. Dominic and Emma remained in the waiting area for another half an hour, hoping Hannah would be able to inform them of any change in his condition.

"I think we should go now, there's nothing we can do by staying here any longer." Dominic stated to Emma after they had spoken to a nurse who had briefly updated them. Emma was reluctant to do so, but knew Dominic was right, even though they had been the cause of this sudden turn of events.

"I hope he's going to be okay, the poor, kind man; I'm to blame," she stammered. "If only I had kept the safe combination numbers with me, none of this would have happened."

They drove back to the gallery; this time, in complete silence. Emma too exhausted with emotion and silently praying for a miracle whilst keeping her fingers crossed at the same time hoping this would expedite the former. And Dominic secretly thinking how fortuitous it would be should the old man die; *that would definitely help solve my plans.*

Chapter Thirteen

Charles had been waiting for them in his office when they arrived back at the gallery. He called Dominic in to speak to him but asked Emma to remain outside. She could tell by their hushed tones that they were ominously discussing the dreadful situation they had unwittingly found themselves involved in.

"Do you think Mr Bloom will survive his heart attack?" Charles questioned Dominic.

"It's not looking good, I must admit, but we got him to the hospital very quickly and they began resuscitating him immediately." Dominic replied, forcing a grim expression for effect.

"This whole situation has become such a mess and the gallery will suffer once word of what's happened reaches public ears; we cannot afford this to occur." Charles stated firmly. "After all, we have taken years to build up our prestigious standing in the art world and to maintain goodwill along with our good *name*." He added, stressing the last word.

Dominic nodding his assent agreed with him and asked, "What shall we do then; to try to recover a modicum of poise and dignity, if that is at all possible?"

"You're not going to like this but after much deliberation, I feel the only way we can move forward is unfortunately to dismiss Emma." He said regrettably. "She was, after all, left in charge of the sketch and as she is still on probation, albeit one more week remaining, I feel this would be the correct decision. What do you think?" He asked, looking to Dominic for support.

"I agree that this has all become untenable but to dismiss Emma, I feel is a bit harsh; she is just young and inexperienced." He replied trying to appear sad and reluctant.

"Well, nevertheless, it has to be done. Please show her in Dominic, I will explain to her gently but firmly our decision." He said with authority.

Emma cautiously entered the office after it had felt like an eternity waiting outside; flashbacks of having to wait outside her headmistress's door came to mind. Thankfully, Helena wasn't around to witness her humiliation as she was gratefully on a day release course for IT and office management at a college in South London. Charles asked her to sit once more in the same seat she had previously sat in; definitely a bad omen she felt, as she knew another lecture was forthcoming. But she certainly didn't expect what she was about to hear.

"With much regret, Emma, I am afraid to tell you that unfortunately, The Hadley Gallery is terminating your employment immediately. We know it has come as a shock to you but for the benefit of the gallery, we felt there wasn't any other choice." While Charles was saying all this, he had been watching Emma closely and wishing this had been unnecessary. Finding it hard to digest the meaning of his speech and unable to comprehend the reason for this decision, she felt the anger welling up inside her and force its way out; like a poison dart aimed to kill.

"I'm just your scapegoat!" she shouted unable to control her emotions. "Blame the new girl after all she's dispensable," she added. Realising she was making a scene and behaving unprofessionally, she tried to calm herself by breathing slowly. But it didn't last as she felt she had been wronged and the injustice of it all brought on the tears, much to her chagrin.

Charles was upset at seeing her so distressed and reiterated that this decision had unfortunately been forced on them. "I will still be able to give you a reference, Emma, after all, before this incident your work here had been exemplary; we were extremely pleased with your progress." With her shoulders still shuddering from sobbing, she shakily stood up and walked out of the room. She had hoped Dominic would have fought her corner but instead he had remained quiet, allowing Charles the distinction of bad cop; with he being the good cop.

She couldn't believe this was happening to her; she had been brought up with the ethos that if you are honest and work hard, you will reap the rewards in life. "Some hopes," she muttered under her breath, "where's it got me, sacked, that's where!" With tears streaming down her face, she robotically closed the books she had been using, knowing she'll not see the fruition of all the work she had lovingly and eagerly put in over the last few months. As she closed the door to her office, she whispered a goodbye to the little room she'd become fond of and had metaphorically grown in.

Charles and Dominic were waiting to escort her from the building. *They do think I'm a criminal, making sure I leave the premises.* She thought to herself. "I expect you're going to search me now?" She blurted out loud this time; as they looked like sentinels guarding a VIP.

At least, they both had the decency to colour-up in response, she thought as she walked to the station. Now what!

Chapter Fourteen

The following morning was in tune with her mood; grey, dismal and pouring with rain. It was the last few days left in October and the clocks had already gone back, making it the end of summer time and the beginning of winter. It couldn't get any worse she felt as she forced herself to get dressed. But instead of eagerly donning a smart outfit fit for the office, she grabbed her jeans and a sweatshirt that she had left over the back of her chair after she had undressed for bed.

Emma discovered she was on her own in the house as her mum had already left for her job, volunteering in their local high-street charity shop. She had stayed in bed a full two hours after waking up recalling all that had been said to her the previous day, until the unfairness and aggravation of it all grudgingly got her out of bed at 11 am. "What am I going to do today?" she thought dejectedly, as she stood looking out the kitchen window into the garden at the puddles forming on the lawn making it look like a swamp.

The day and her mood didn't alter, in fact it became worse; as she could hear the rumble of thunder coming closer as the skies darkened and the rain lashed down in torrents against the windows. Suddenly, a flash of lightening brightened up the room and jolted her out of her lethargy as if she'd been given an electric shock. It sparked a feeling of injustice in her and infused a determination to improve her awful situation. "It's no good; me mooning around the house that won't achieve anything," she admonished. Still reproaching herself, she picked up her mobile phone and dialled Alice's number. She hoped Alice would be able to speak as she knew she was still at work in the travel agency.

"Hello," Alice thankfully answered. "Are you at work, Emma?" She added. Emma shook her head then realised she needed to speak; "No, I've been dismissed." She replied dreading the response.

"Goodness, why what has happened?" Alice alarmingly asked.

"Can we meet up later; then I'll be able to tell you everything." Emma suggested.

"Of course, I'll come straight from work and meet you in Café Rouge in the high street near to you in Ruislip. Is 6.30, okay? Then you can fill me in." Emma agreed and was looking forward to unburdening herself to her caring friend.

Fortunately, the worse of the weather was over by the time Emma was ready to leave for her rendezvous with Alice. In fact, at around 4 pm, the sun had made a brief appearance after the violent thunderstorm had cleared the air. There were still a few angry-looking clouds around, so the threat that it might rain again prompted Emma to collect her umbrella from the coat stand in the hall as she put on her raincoat. Her mum had gone food shopping after finishing her shift at the charity shop and had informed Emma she wouldn't be home before she would have left to meet her friend. But had wished her a nice time and hoped to see her later so they could have an overdue catch-up.

Emma decided to walk to the high street as it would only take her about half an hour and wouldn't be worth catching a bus. Anyway, the walk would help clear her mind before bombarding poor Alice with all her woes. She wished she had put on a warmer coat though, as a cool breeze had blown in as soon as it became dark without her realising it; "winter is on its way," she muttered, and then remembered gratefully, that she had left a scarf in her raincoat pocket.

She peered into the café window but was unable to see whether Alice was inside as the windows were partially steamed up. It was definitely too chilly now to wait outside as she had begun shivering; possibly from lack of food; she realised she hadn't eaten all day, as well as being genuinely cold. She sat down at a table easily visible from the street so that Alice would be able to see her immediately. It didn't seem too long before Alice arrived just as Emma was studying the menu. After greeting each other warmly, they both decided that they needed to order something to eat and drink before any serious analysis of Emma's current situation should begin.

The food definitely did the trick as Emma's stomach growled to confirm its appreciation on being fed. Feeling stronger and more animated so that she would be able to clearly recall the events leading up to her dismissal without becoming too emotional, she opened her heart out to her dear friend. Not wanting her to lose her flow, Alice interjected occasionally unable to believe all that Emma had been through since she last saw her. "You poor thing, you don't deserve all this distress, it will make you ill." She said, angry at the treatment her friend had received. "I *know* how trustworthy you are and that you wouldn't dream of doing anything dishonest, so forget them and move on." She said hoping she didn't sound too abrupt.

"How can I move on when there's an elderly man lying in hospital because of me?" Emma miserably stated with tears threatening to form.

"Stop this!" Alice urged as she could see what was happening. "There's a vacancy where I work for a travel agent, why not apply? It'll help you to focus on something else." Alice suggested, trying to raise Emma's mood again.

"I think you're right; it will do me good; I'll call in tomorrow, thanks, Alice. I knew I could rely on you to help me."

The following day with the early autumn sun shining, along with a more positive outlook, Emma hopped on the tube to take her to Northolt and then made her way to Alice's place of work. Alice had paved the way with her manager beforehand, so she was expecting Emma. After the formal introductions were completed, Emma handed Mrs Hargreaves, the reference letter from Charles as was requested when she had phoned.

"Alice has given you a glowing report, Emma, so I hope you won't let me down if I offer you a position on our customer sales team." Janet Hargreaves asked and looked to Emma for reassurance.

"Thank you, I need this job and I look forward to being part of your sales team; when do I start?" She said eagerly.

"Why, tomorrow if that's all right with you, we're very busy now, bookings are coming in thick and fast for winter skiing holidays and I hear from Alice that you and her have had experience in that field, am I correct?" She said with a wry smile.

"Yes most definitely!" Emma beamed, and she felt her world had suddenly become slightly brighter.

Chapter Fifteen

Monday, 1 November 1999

When Helena had been informed by Charles that Emma had been dismissed, outwardly, she had appeared shocked and upset. Secretly, she was overjoyed that all her efforts at discrediting Emma had been worth it and her devious plan had come to fruition. Not that she really had hated Emma, she thought, but the fun of being able to manipulate people and events excited her and empowered her. She was just peeved that she hadn't been there that day to witness her departure.

Dominic had texted her that morning for her to meet him at the outside café in the centre of Covent Garden at lunchtime, as he urgently needed to speak to her. She hadn't felt like going into work as she was feeling lazy and couldn't be bothered even to let them know. She would much rather go shopping, so meeting Uncle Dominic would suit her perfectly; she'd be able to spend the rest of the afternoon at the shops and market stalls.

It was typically November weather, as well as being the first Monday in the month; drizzly and miserably cold, consequently, dripping umbrellas were forcing pedestrians into the kerb to dodge being poked in the head by them. Being lunchtime, the place was crowded as it was undercover and customers were competing with the sparrows and pigeons for a table. The queue for food stretched out of the café area and encroached into the marketplace. Helena didn't want to stay here to eat, so as soon as Dominic arrived, they went down the steps to a smaller café on the ground floor; where a trio of musicians were hoping to raise money as well as people's spirits.

"I didn't arrange to meet you here for pleasure, Helena." Dominic stated firmly. The omelettes they had ordered arrived just as he finished speaking.

"Why did you want to see me, then?" Helena questioned and took a mouthful of the overcooked, rubbery looking food. "Yuk, this is cold and disgusting. I'm not eating this!" She exclaimed pushing the plate away.

"Then don't! I'm not bothered or interested in your likes or dislikes." Dominic replied angrily. "What I want from you now is the receipt to be able to recover the sketch from the pawnbroker; it's been a few weeks since you left it with him, so it's time to redeem it without arousing any suspicion."

"Okay, but I've left it in my other bag, the one I used to take it in. You'll have to wait until tomorrow and I'll bring it into work." She shrugged.

"As long as you deign to come into work tomorrow and don't forget it either!" He added stressing the last word. "I'm going now." He left the money on the table for their meal, then stood up and walked away, leaving Helena feeling disgruntled.

At home that evening, Helena went to get the Hermès bag she had thrown into her wardrobe. The last time she had used it was to carry the sketch to the pawnbroker; it seemed ages ago now. She emptied the contents onto her bed and an avalanche of used tickets, old wrappers as well as make-up and a brush she thought she had lost, spilled out. She searched for the receipt for the sketch amongst the detritus but couldn't find it. She remembered stuffing it into her bag with the money the pawnbroker gave her. "Where can it be?" she said out loud. "It has to be here!" she stressed and searched through everything again, convinced she'll find it. But there was no sign of it. Her mind was blank as she was trying to recall all her movements on that day. The only thing that could possibly have happened was when she had taken the money out of her bag to pay for the boots she had bought, perhaps the receipt had fallen out without her noticing. "God, what am I going to say to Uncle Dominic?" she cried, knowing she'll be in a lot of trouble.

When she told him the following day, he was livid. It was fitting that they were in Emma's old office when he figuratively exploded at her incompetence. "You're a complete idiot, Helena. I should never have trusted you. Now what am I going to do?" He shouted at her. "The pawnbroker has every right to sell any article that has not been redeemed at any price he chooses. And once he knows the true value of it, he'll bump up the price extortionately." Worriedly, he slumped down into the nearest chair dismayed and annoyed at the situation he had allowed to happen.

"All we can possibly do is for both of us to go there and see if he will hand it over without a receipt. After all, I'll be giving him back the £900 plus any interest that might have accrued, and hopefully he should also remember you with a bit of luck." After he had decided on this course of action, Dominic's mood drastically altered; he felt reassured and confident that this was just a hiccup and that his plan to own the sketch nefariously, was still on track.

Chapter Sixteen

The first week at the travel agency flew by quickly for Emma as she was too engrossed in learning about a sector she had never worked in before. By the second week, however, she realised this wasn't going to be her true vocation in life. It was fine as a standby for being able to earn a salary, but her passion and commitment was for the art world, most definitely. The one advantage for her working there, apart from a wage packet, was that she was with Alice. On quieter days, they were able to have lunch together; providing the weather was amenable, they walked to the nearby park and ate their sandwiches huddled under the bandstand. It gave them a chance to catch up generally on each other's lives and to be free of the office at the same time.

On one of these days, Emma voiced her feelings to her friend. "I'm grateful to you, Alice, for helping me get this job but I know it's really not where I had envisaged my life to be at this point. I do miss the gallery." Alice listened sympathetically and she could see how Emma was still upset at being badly treated by Dominic but she couldn't understand why she wanted to be back there. From how Emma had described his coldness towards her after charming her into his bed, it was mortifying to see her dear friend still besotted with him. He had even supported his brother wholeheartedly on having Emma dismissed.

"You need to take your rose-tinted glasses off now, and see Dominic for the chauvinistic man he really was; you were useful to him and that was all." She said, hoping Emma would understand her harsh diatribe. Shrugging her shoulders in acknowledgement to Alice's well-meaning words, she knew she was right and wished she could forget him. They made their way back to work in relative silence, both reflecting on their last conversation.

"Would you come with me to visit Mr Bloom in hospital after work tonight, Alice?" Emma asked as they were opening the shop door. "I owe it to him to see if he is all right. I really liked him and I hope he'll agree to me visiting him."

"Of course, I will." Alice smiled, pleased that her friend had brightened up. "We'll buy some grapes from the convenience store in the high street on the way." She added.

It had been raining steadily all afternoon, so by the time they were ready to leave work, the pavements were like an assault course with people jumping over large puddles to avoid splashing themselves. Emma and Alice were sharing the same umbrella as Alice had kindly lent hers to a colleague who had been without one. They were laughing at the antics of people trying to cross the road without being sprayed by the muddy water the cars were churning up, when they stopped under the awning of a pawnbroker's shop for respite. Emma was busy shaking out the umbrella from any excess rain and trying to avoid soaking any passers-by at the same time, as Alice who had momentarily glanced into the shop window called Emma over. Following in the direction of where Alice's finger was pointing, Emma was stunned to see, sitting propped up behind a porcelain figurine of an Edwardian lady with a basket of posies over one arm, the Klimt sketch of *The Kiss*. Speechless, she turned to Alice and began stuttering unable to believe what she was seeing. "It can't be; surely, it must be a replica. If it isn't, how would it have ended up here?" She questioned in amazement. "I need to look at it more closely, but it's too late now, the shop is closed for the night."

They knew they didn't have any choice but to reluctantly leave the sketch there and continue on to buy the grapes for Mr Bloom and then to return the next day when the shop will hopefully be open to them. On the way to the hospital, all they could talk about was whether the item in the pawnbroker's window was the real sketch and how, if it was, would they be able to buy it. There were so many questions wanting answers that in the end, the confusion drained her energy and gave Emma a headache which she hoped wouldn't turn into a migraine. She felt a slight relief, when at having reached the admissions ward to be told that Viktor Bloom had been discharged and sent home that same day as they had been satisfied with his progress. Although it had been a wasted journey for them both, at least she knew that he had recovered and was well enough to go home and be with his Hannah.

Exhausted from everything that had materialised that evening, they both decided that the need to be home quickly was paramount to their well-being, so with that in mind, they hailed a black cab that had been waiting in the nearby taxi rank just outside the hospital. Gratefully, they sank into the cab's comfortable leather seats and allowed the driver to escort them to their respective homes. Tomorrow, they'll go to the shop in their lunchtime, and hopefully uncover the true identity of the sketch. The last thought Emma had as she climbed into her bed that night was an image of the 'The Kiss' sitting forlornly on a dusty, dark shelf inside a dingy pawnbroker's shop instead of in a prestigious art gallery, where it should rightfully be; it was as if it was calling out to her to be rescued.

Chapter Seventeen

Eager to get to work and to see Alice, Emma hurriedly got showered and dressed before even her mum had risen. She'd had a fitful sleep and dreamt all of her clothes were being stolen from her wardrobe and she had been helpless to prevent it; *strange how the mind works*, she thought. Walking the short distance from the station to work gave her time to formulate an idea on how to approach the pawnbroker. But as she got nearer to the travel agency, she could see a police car had parked outside, directly next to the kerb and in front of the shop. She cautiously opened the door unsure of what she would be met with.

"Ah, Miss Fogle, I've been waiting to speak with you." It was the young police constable who had interviewed her immediately after the sketch had gone missing. Out of the corner of her eye, Emma could see her manager, Janet Hargreaves quizzically looking in her direction. Ignoring her manager's angry body language, Emma smiled at the policeman and said, "I'm sorry, can I help you, constable?"

"Unfortunately, we need to interview you again concerning the theft of the artwork that was last seen in your possession; some other evidence has come to light. It is necessary for you to accompany me now to the police station."

Before she had time to explain anything to anyone, she was escorted out of the shop and into the awaiting police car. Alice witnessed her friend's humiliation and felt helpless. She could see that her manager was furious with the scene that Emma had unwittingly created and she knew this would ultimately affect her employment. At least, there hadn't been any customers present as it was still quite early; surely that will go in her favour, Alice hoped.

Emma was shown into an interview room as soon as they arrived at the station. She was offered a glass of water as she looked very pale and her hands were shaking; causing her to spill some of the contents onto her trousers. She wondered why she was being held in this dingy, grey, bare room with just the standard tea-stained wood table between her and the two policemen sitting opposite her; one being the young constable and the other, an older version but with a cultivated stubble around his chin. She was not a criminal! With this thought in her head, it gave her the strength and determination to question her accusers. "Why have you brought me here? I told you everything two weeks ago!"

"Well, Emma, we've had an anonymous tip off that you were seen that night carrying the stolen artwork out of the gallery and the description they gave us does fit your profile. What have you got to say regarding this new information?" The older one of the two asked and stared directly into her eyes waiting for her reply.

"I would like to know *who* fed you this utter rubbish, probably the same person who actually did steal it, I expect." She replied indignantly. "Nothing has changed from my original statement and I'm as eager as you to identify the real culprit." Emma added for good measure. She was going to tell them about the sighting in the pawnbroker's window the previous evening, but thought better of it in case they suspected her of leaving it there; that's if, it was the real masterpiece. After two hours and seemingly satisfied with her answers to their questioning, they allowed her to go but implied that she might be required to 'help' them with any further enquiries, should anything else arise. She knew they couldn't have any substantial evidence on her otherwise they wouldn't have given up so quickly.

Relieved to be out of there, Emma made her way back to work, hoping that she wouldn't be in too much trouble, but that was wishful thinking. As she entered the shop, she could see a young couple sitting at Alice's desk studying holiday brochures and asking for her advice on which hotel they should book in the Algarve. Alice looked up when she saw Emma walk back in, but unable to speak to her, she gave her a questioning look instead. Janet Hargreaves had heard the bell over the door, chime, when Emma had opened it and was marching towards her. "Don't bother removing your coat," she snapped, "I do *not* want any further visits from the police and obviously, you invite trouble. I'm very disappointed that I trusted you and thought you would fit in here perfectly; obviously, I was very much mistaken. You'll be paid what you are owed as you are no longer employed here." After saying that, she turned and walked back into her office leaving Emma astonished as yet again, within two weeks she had had the misfortune of being fired twice. What on earth was happening to her!

She walked over to the park as she wasn't sure where else to go. She had to gather her thoughts and to assess this new dilemma. There was a chilly breeze and she pulled her white, knitted pompom hat firmly over her ears for extra warmth and wound the matching scarf more tightly round her neck. The trees were becoming bare after shedding their worn-out suits of reds, yellows and oranges with squirrels running furiously amongst them; each one on a mission to bury any acorns or chestnuts in the hope of remembering where to find their stock of food come winter. Emma watched nature carrying on regardless of any other interruptions and knew she should do exactly the same. "Learn from the best," she whispered to herself.

Feeling stronger from her refreshing walk, she made her way back the way she came and judging it must be nearly lunchtime, she texted Alice to make her aware that she was outside waiting for her. She peered tentatively through the glass of the shop door hoping to see Alice collecting her coat and bag ready to join her outside, but she was horrified to witness her friend remonstrating with Janet Hargreaves probably over her dismissal. Alice burst through the door before Emma could move fully out of her way and almost caused her to over balance.

"I'm so sorry, Emma, if I nearly knocked you over but I'm so angry. I tried explaining that none of this was your fault but she wouldn't listen to any reasoning. I almost told her what she could do with her job, but thought better of it; otherwise, we would both have been out of work." Alice said trying to take deep breaths so as to calm herself.

"Look, Alice, I really appreciate your loyalty to me but please don't give your notice in on my account, you need this job or how else will you be able to afford your rent?" She said and then added, "There are not enough park benches for us both to sleep on and I'm not sharing." Laughing at this, the two friends linked arms and headed for the nearest café for a sandwich, a hot mug of tea and perhaps a slice of cake, if it was available. Once seated, and in between mouthfuls, Emma related to Alice her journey to the police station and the questioning she received. "I'm sure they're convinced that I'm the thief and apparently an unknown witness verifies this *and* I'm not to leave the country. Great! What hope have I got!"

Now feeling replete from their lunch, Alice checked her watch and informed Emma that they would still have time to get to the pawnbroker before she would have to return to work. Emma agreed they should go immediately as too much time had already been wasted on unforeseen complications that had delayed their plans. They walked just another fifty yards before reaching their destination and then stopped in front of the same window as they had done the previous evening. It wasn't there! "We're too late! Surely, we didn't imagine it, did we?" Emma exclaimed. "Let's go inside and find out." She said and pushed the door open with a force she was unaware of.

A musty atmosphere inside clung to their nostrils; the whole place looked like it had come straight out of a Dickens novel. When the proprietor came forward from behind a shabby curtain, this seemed to confirm their thoughts as he was the epitome of a Scrooge look-a-like character.

"Good afternoon, ladies, how can I help you?" He asked politely. Emma explained in detail the sketch they thought they had seen in his window, but now, as it was no longer there, perhaps they had been mistaken.

"No, you were correct, there *was* a drawing on the shelf last night. It had only been in the window for one day before someone came in and purchased it." He said with a smile at remembering the amount of money he had received for selling it. "I do have other paintings you might be interested in; mainly landscapes though." He added, hoping he might get another lucrative sale; two in one day would be a record, he thought.

"No, we were only interested in that one you had. I know it might be unethical to ask you, but could you describe to us who you sold it to? It would help us greatly." She pleaded and then gave him her sweetest smile hoping he would comply.

He shrugged his shoulders and said it didn't make any difference to him and gave them a full description of a well-dressed gentleman in his forties accompanied by a young girl who referred to him as her uncle. He had recognised the girl, he said, as she had originally brought the drawing in to be pawned but had lost her receipt. He hoped this information was of help to them and then said if they did not wish to purchase anything, he must get back to his work and bidding them goodbye, he turned and retreated behind his curtain once again.

"Good God!" Emma exclaimed to Alice once they were standing outside. "You know what this means? He has unbelievably described Dominic and Helena as the customers. I knew Helena didn't like me but why would she involve her uncle in her deceit? Something is definitely wrong and I've got to become as devious as her to discover the truth and somehow to retrieve the sketch."

Chapter Eighteen

That same morning, Dominic was waiting in his car for Helena to arrive. It was still quite early; the dashboard clock read 8.30 am. He had pre-arranged with her to meet with him at the top of her road at 9.00 am. She was to tell her parents that she was meeting with some friends from school that she hadn't seen since she had left last year, and they would be having breakfast out; this would help explain her need to leave the house unusually early, something she would rarely, if *ever* do. She had made it sound even more convincing by adding that they would be going on a shopping spree afterwards, and therefore, would naturally need some extra 'pocket money' for her not to feel inferior as her friends were from wealthier families. She had calculated this remark would hit a nerve and she would be rewarded with more than she had originally asked for; as they 'wanted her to enjoy her day'. She revelled in using psychological tactics on her parents, *it always worked*, she smugly thought.

Dominic looked at his watch, it was nearly 9.00 am and there was still no sign of her in the street. Fuming at her tardiness, he decided to text her to hurry her up. He had emphasised to her the importance of being early as he had wanted to be at the pawnbroker's as the shop opened. He hoped his brother hadn't been near her when she had read the text as he didn't want her to have to answer any awkward questions and catch her 'off guard'.

As he looked up from his mobile phone, he could see her dawdling towards the car as if time wasn't of the essence. Winding his window down, he called out to her to hurry herself. In response, she pulled a face at him, like a baby suffering with wind. She opened the car door and whilst yawning so that her tonsils were visible as she hadn't bothered to cover her mouth, she slumped into the seat next to him.

"I need you to be alert, not still half asleep." He said irritated by her unfeminine conduct. "You're the only one who knows where we're going and

I'll be needing directions as soon as we get nearer to Northolt as I'm not familiar with that area." He added.

"You worry too much, so chill out or you'll have a heart attack, like that old man you purloined the sketch from." Helena said without feeling and closed her eyes hoping to grab a few minutes of extra sleep.

He nudged her to wake up as they were approaching the town; there was a one-way system and he wasn't sure of the best place to park the car. Helena directed him to the car park she had previously used as it seemed the nearest one to their destination.

"Let me do most of the talking as we need to be convincing." Dominic whispered to Helena as they opened the door and walked inside the shop. They had seen the Klimt sketch propped up on a shelf in the window as they had stood outside, and now all they had to do was persuade the proprietor and maybe barter with him, and then the sketch would be theirs.

"Good morning, you *are* early birds, I have only just opened." Smiling and showing uneven brown stained teeth, he added, "How can I help you?"

"Unbeknown to me," Dominic began and pointing to Helena at the same time said, "my niece brought a drawing of mine here last month. In fact, it is now in your window and I need to have it back. Unfortunately, she has lost the receipt you gave her but I'm sure you must recognise her."

Peering at Helena over the top of his spectacles, he frowned, "Oh yes, I remember her but it's against the shop policy for an article to be redeemed without one. I'm sorry but you may not be bona fide, I will need proof of who you claim to be." He said adamantly. Dominic produced a business card from his jacket and hoped this would alleviate any doubts. The older man nodded in agreement after he had studied the card Dominic had presented to him. After handing Dominic's card back to him and feeling partially satisfied, he then went to retrieve the sketch from his window display. He placed it down onto the counter as if it was an old photograph of no particular value. But he could see now how Dominic's eyes lit up and knew this man, standing in front of him, had desperately wanted this drawing to be returned to him, so it must be worth much more than he initially thought. With this in his mind, he looked squarely at Dominic, "Because I'm now within my rights to sell any article that is without a receipt, you will need to pay me £2000 if you wish to purchase it."

"But my niece told me you gave her £900 initially. I expected to pay some interest on that amount, but I feel you are very much overcharging me." Dominic knew this new price was extremely reasonable considering it was purported to be a genuine Klimt, but obviously this old man didn't have a clue to its value, and he was even prepared to go up to £3000 just to get it back and smiled to himself. After some timely deliberation, Dominic said, "Okay, I will agree to that figure," and counted out the money in £50 notes so as none of the money would be traceable back to him. Taking the money Dominic had placed on the counter, the older man handed him the drawing and thanked him for doing business with him. Grinning, he watched them leave and congratulated himself on achieving the best sale he'd had for a long while and wished every morning could be the same.

"Well, that was painless. I thought it went quite smoothly, don't you?" Dominic asked Helena.

"Oh, am I allowed to talk now?" She chided.

"Just be thankful I have it back in my possession. After all, you gained from it or have you forgotten the £900 you spent frivolously?" Not expecting her to answer and with the prized art work now in his briefcase, he was already formulating in his mind his next plan to recover some of the £40,000 he had lost at the casino the previous week. *You lose some then you win some*; that was his life.

Chapter Nineteen

Still reeling from losing two jobs in less than a month, Emma wondered if she was just very unlucky or extremely careless. Now that she had the time to devote all her energies into trying to rescue her beloved sketch; well, actually, Mr Bloom's beloved sketch, she didn't want the hassle of searching for any new employment just yet. Not that she had the inclination to do that either.

She had tried telling her mum about the events that had led up to her dismissal but it had become too complicated, and she became aware of her mother's eyes starting to glaze over and of her stifling a yawn. She knew she should inform the police of the latest developments but she still didn't have any actual proof that Dominic and Helena were the perpetrators. Somehow, she felt, it was going to be her responsibility to finally unravel this conundrum as she knew, in her heart, she had been part guilty; *if only the clock could be turned back to that evening when I inadvertently left the safe numbers for all and sundry to find*, and then cringed at her own stupidity.

First and foremost, I must go to visit Mr Bloom to see if he has fully recovered, she urged herself. *I need to be proactive and regardless of whether he might refuse to see me; after all, due to my incompetence, the poor man ended up in hospital. I owe it to him to do the right thing and forget my own feelings.* It definitely helped her to talk outwardly to herself even though, when she was on her own, it made sense, and gave her the encouragement she needed. She knew she had to be brave and go alone as Alice would be at work and there had been no chance of asking her to take a day's leave to accompany her after the kerfuffle yesterday.

For once, the sun was shining after a week of constant rain; *perhaps, this is a good omen*, Emma thought to herself. It brightened her mood and she felt confident she'd made the right decision to visit him after all. She wanted to make a good impression and she knew he had an eye for beautiful things, so she wore her new cobalt blue wool coat with matching beret and gloves and hoped he would see she was trying to appease him. "I just hope he will be well enough to appreciate my effort," she whispered to herself.

It was just before lunch by the time Emma reached his house in Finchley; the journey had taken longer than she had anticipated as she'd had to find her way there by public transport. The only other times she had been there was with Dominic in his car. The thought of him and how she had trusted him made her shiver with anger. "Focus on *now*!" she sharply reminded herself and pressed the bell fixed to the door frame. No one answered, and so, after a few minutes, she lifted the brass door-knocker and used it to knock twice; she heard the sound echo in the hallway behind the front door. "I hope someone is in after plucking up the courage to be here," she thought. Finally, she could hear advancing footsteps and her heart began racing at the thought she might be about to receive an unpleasant confrontation. The door opened wide and Hannah stood still, staring at Emma with disbelief and then frowned, obviously remembering the previous time she had visited and started to close the door in her face.

"Hannah, please don't shut the door! I need to know how Mr Bloom is." Emma cried with urgency. "Is he feeling much better so that I can talk with him?" She knew she was pleading with Hannah but she had to make her realise that her intentions were honest. After giving Emma a long, scrutinising look, the other woman said, "You'd better come in," and opened the door further to allow her to enter the hallway.

Emma admired Hannah for her loyalty to Viktor Bloom; she was like a sentry guarding the inner sanctum of royalty. She also wondered if there was a hint of affection or perhaps, even love for the elderly man. Nevertheless, she knew they respected each other and *she* needed to gain Hannah's respect herself.

"Mr Bloom is resting at the moment but I shall tell him you are here. Wait here, please." And she turned and opened the door to the familiar room where Emma and Dominic had been twice before. After ten minutes, Hannah emerged, "He said he is sorry to keep you waiting but he has only just woken up and if you'd be so kind to allow him another five minutes for him to gather his thoughts." She relayed his exact words to her. He was such a gentleman and Emma could vividly imagine him speaking so appropriately and felt honoured that he hadn't refused to meet with her.

"Please ask her to come in," she heard him say to Hannah. Escorted, she followed Hannah into the room. The cluttered table, still with books and brochures on it, had been pushed against the longest wall opposite the French doors to make room for a day bed; similar to a chaise longue but with three sides made from decorated wrought iron for support. Viktor Bloom was sitting propped up by several pillows, with his legs stretched out and covered with a beautiful tartan wool blanket in autumn shades of oranges and browns.

"How are you Mr Bloom?" Emma asked gingerly. "I'm so pleased that you are looking so much better now." She added remembering his deathly pallor the last time she saw him.

"They say I am on the right recovery road but have still further to travel." He replied with a shrug and an impish smile. "But why are you here, Emma?"

"I needed to talk to you about everything that has happened and to put you in the picture, please excuse the pun." She said with a little embarrassment. "But if you are not strong enough at the moment, I am able to return another time, if that would suit you better?"

"No, please pull up a chair and sit down near to me so that I can hear you clearly," he said. "By the way, Emma, you look very smart and such a beautiful colour." He said admiring her coat. "But please remove it, otherwise you won't feel the benefit when you go out." He added wisely.

Hannah busied herself overseeing the logistics of removing the chair of its magazines and papers to allow Emma to sit down and to pull the chair closer. "I'll make a pot of tea for you both," she said efficiently and walked out of the room allowing them time together. Plucking up her courage, she began to relate to Viktor, he insisted on her using his first name, everything that had happened to her, including seeing his beloved sketch in the pawnbroker's window. He was shocked when she told him who she thought the couple were who had claimed it and had then 'pipped' her at the post the previous day. She was worried that she might have caused him to become too stressed with all her news and didn't want to weaken his progress.

It was as if she could lift her head up again after freeing herself from the torrent of words coursing out of her, like a swollen river that had burst through a dam. The emotion and relief of having someone understand all that she had been through left her in floods of tears. She was grateful when Hannah brought in the tea so that she could compose herself and allow Viktor to speak. He had patiently listened to her throughout, without any interruptions. "So, Emma," he finally spoke out quietly after absorbing all this new information, "what is your next step? I'm too old to help you other than to inform the police. But you say you need more proof for that, but how to get it?" He said shrugging his shoulders and opening his hands in a gesture to perhaps a higher entity.

"What if we hired a private detective to follow him?" She suggested as the idea had suddenly come to her.

"That's possible," he replied and then added, "but whom?"

"Let me think about it, but we have to act quickly in case he decides to sell it on; that man has no scruples at all."

Hannah came into the room carrying Viktor's lunch on a tray and had overheard the end of their conversation. She asked Emma to briefly enlighten her as she was concerned for Viktor's well-being and wouldn't want him to have a 'set-back'. "I didn't trust *him* from the start as he wouldn't look me in the eyes whenever he spoke to me." She said emphasising strongly about Dominic. "I did warn Viktor but he pooh-poohed it and said I was being overcautious as he trusted you completely; as you reminded him of someone from years ago." Smiling at Emma, she asked if she would also like a bowl of chicken soup as she had made it freshly that morning and there was plenty of it. Viktor nodded at her to take up Hannah's offer as it was his favourite soup and he knew she would enjoy it. It warmed Emma to realise that this meant she had been accepted as a friend and that they had believed her.

"That was absolutely delicious, thank you." Emma exclaimed as Hannah cleared the empty bowls back onto the tray. "I don't think I've ever known a soup to be so nourishing and satisfying." She added. Hannah laughed, "It's an old Jewish recipe that has been handed down from generations and made with love."

Feeling happier now, despite the news Emma had brought to him, Viktor asked Hannah if she wouldn't mind fetching the old, brown cardboard box down from his bedroom containing all his family's ancient photos. There was one in particular that he would like to show Emma. Obligingly, Hannah went to fetch it for him; she knew she would *even* get the top brick off the chimney for him, if he asked her for it. Rummaging through it, after Hannah had placed it next to him onto a side table, he was determined to find it. He knew in his mind's eye, that he remembered it as being very small and in sepia as it was extremely old. After sifting through so many and occasionally describing to Emma their various meanings and along with his description of his childhood, a picture of his life began to emerge. At last, quite near to the bottom of the box, he found it, tucked inside a yellowing envelope.

It was a photograph of Viktor's father, Berret with Emilie; the beautifully striking auburn-haired model portrayed in Gustav Klimt's painting of 'The Kiss'. Viktor's father had kept it secretly from his wife all the time they had been married, Viktor explained. He had given it to his son when he knew he was dying and had requested him to also keep his secret. It had apparently been taken by Klimt as an experiment after he had acquired this new German photographic machine called a Voigtländer camera. It was one of the first photos taken in the studio and the reason why he so treasured it.

"But I want you to take a good look at Emilie and tell me who she reminds you of." He asked Emma and carefully passed her the photo. Gently taking it from him, she studied the woman and a strange feeling swept over her. "How can it possibly be? She looks uncannily like me or should I say, I look uncannily like her." Emma whispered in disbelief.

"That was why I needed to see the photo once again." Viktor confirmed. "When I first saw you with that man, Dominic Hadley, I felt a connection to you but I was unable to recollect the reason why. But, seeing you again today made me remember this photo. I don't know what this all means except that you are also a beautiful young woman." Along with the photo, Viktor had also kept an old newspaper cutting from Vienna that his cousin had sent to him; it was a report of the death of Emilie Louise Flöge in 1952 and a brief eulogy of her having been Gustav Klimt's lover. Emma read the fading print avidly and the connection she felt was momentous; not only did she have a similar first and surname but her middle name was identical.

"I would love to have a copy of it, if I may? Somehow, I feel empathy towards Emilie as if she is calling out to me and I would like to research her and get to know her better."

Hannah said she would get a copy of both the photo and the newspaper cutting for her as they really didn't want to let it out of their sight, not that they didn't trust *her*. Emma totally understood their reservations and agreed with them. Emma could see Viktor was now looking exhausted and she knew it was time for her to go. "I will be back soon with hopefully some good news but I will keep you informed either way." She said putting on her coat. "Thank you both for being so kind and understanding." Opening the door, Hannah smiled and wished her well.

That night asleep in her bed, Emma had a vivid dream that she had become Emilie Flöge and was being embraced just as the painting depicted her; dressed in a flamboyant flowing dress, with flowers scattered in her hair and kneeling so very close to her lover. She sighed not wanting her dream to end.

detective dealing with their case greeted them and all three were then shown into a private room. He spoke in English for Emma's benefit.

"You will be pleased to know that we have been able to trace the number plate of the car in question even though we didn't have the full details." He explained in stilted English. "It is a hired car but we have already spoken to the company and they were able to give us the name of the person who had rented it. As he is a Hungarian citizen, we have had to inform their police department in Budapest of our intention to pay him a visit. This might delay things slightly as they are not too happy that we, in Vienna, are involved."

"So, does that mean my friend Alice is being held prisoner somewhere in Hungary?" Emma said alarmingly. "Please, please do all you can to get her back, I beg of you!"

"We will be going there today as soon as we get confirmation from their department." He strongly assured them. "We will keep you informed of any developments."

They said goodbye to Joseph and thanked him profusely for helping them get this far. "Just call me if you need me again." He had kindly said to them.

"Are you beginning to feel better now?" Karl asked her as they got into the car.

"I am, but I have had an idea. What if we go ourselves to Budapest as we might be able to find out something and not waste any more time? What do you think?" Emma said hoping he would agree with her sudden change of plan.

His reply to her was to turn his car around into the direction of Budapest, roughly a two-hour journey away. He knew she would want to be involved and not leave it just to the police to solve. He hadn't known her for long but he was already able to read her mind.

The journey there gave Emma a chance to take stock of the whole situation from the start to hopefully, let it be soon, the end. *It was hard to believe* she thought to herself, *that if she hadn't taken the job with The Hadley, Alice and she would still be happy living a mundane existence without any hope of excitement. But this is going to the absolute extreme! So much had happened; holding that wonderful, magical sketch and then losing it, falling for Dominic and then he showing his true colours and was shot for it, and my poor, lovely Alice being abducted.* All these thoughts and scenarios were buzzing in her mind, like a confused bee with too many flowers to pollinate.

Arriving in Budapest, Emma could see it would have been an interesting city for her to explore under better circumstances. The spires of the gothic churches stood proud above the historical buildings. They decided though, to head straight for the main central police station and hoped they would be communicative and relatively friendly towards her and Karl.

Unfortunately, they were met with indifference and had shrugged when Emma had stressed the plight her friend was in. Behind their false smiles, Emma could detect an arrogant, cold, hardness and had wanted to shout at them for not caring; but as she didn't want to be locked up, she had thought better of it. They had been standing beside the admissions officer's desk from the time they had entered and had not had the courtesy of being asked to sit down. She knew they were wasting their time expecting any assistance, and in her impatience to leave, she overbalanced and her bag accidently knocked over, what looked like a mug of cold coffee, all over a file of papers that had been left open on the desk.

The false smiles quickly vanished and had been replaced with angry words; which fortunately Emma didn't understand but she was able to guess at. "I'm so sorry," she said unconvincingly and offered to help mop up the mess. She was pushed aside as the officer opened the top drawer of his desk to recover a cloth for the purpose. In the corner of the drawer, Emma saw a digital camera with a note attached to it by a rubber band. She glanced at the two names written on the note; one of them was Alice's! The officer had closed the drawer before he had gone to dispose of the wet cloth. Taking the opportunity, she quickly opened the drawer, grabbed the camera and ran out of the police station with a bemused Karl following closely behind her.

"I can't believe you just did that; you actually stole from the police!" Karl laughed as they ran to the car. "We're just borrowing it and it's mine anyway! It's their fault; they should have been more helpful." She said out of breath from running and laughing. "It's a means to an end." She added.

"Stop the car!" She shouted at Karl. Startled, he instantly pulled into a side road. They had been heading for the city outskirts, as far away from the police station as possible in case their misdemeanour had already been discovered. "What is the matter?" he asked.

Emma had unwound the note and was looking through the camera. She could now comprehend what Alice had been through in the last 48 hours. She showed Karl the images of both men in the casino and inside Dominic's hotel room. Alice had been meticulous taking many photos as evidence; including a shaky one of

Dominic after he had been shot and before Alice had been discovered hiding on the balcony. Scrolling further along, they saw the images Alice had cleverly taken from the window of her prison. And that was the last one. "What has happened to her since? Where can she be?" Again, Emma repeated the same questions to Karl hoping for a positive answer.

Chapter Thirty

Once her abductors had left the barn, and had checked to make sure Alice was still deep in a supposedly drugged-induced sleep, she went over to the spot where they had been and began heaving aside the heavy hay bales. It was quite difficult as they were bulky and she was small and not that strong. The spikes of the straw were cutting into her fingers and making them bleed, but much worse was the fact that all her manicured nails had been broken in the task. "Never mind once this nightmare is over, I'll be able to treat myself again to a spa and manicure, the full treatment!" She reasoned, forcing herself to be positive and trying to infuse some levity into the bleakness.

Tugging hard to dislodge the last bale, she fell backwards and hit her head on the stone floor. It stunned her momentarily and she sat still to recover until the coldness of the ground started to seep into her clothing; making her realise she was still wearing the trousers and angora jumper which had been unsuitable for the casino, for not being dressier and even less suitable for being held captive in, as not being warm enough and were now both grubby and dishevelled. "I must smell!" the thought appalled her.

Focusing back on the area she had just managed to clear; she could see she had uncovered two large suitcases. She tried to force them open but they had been securely locked. "This being a barn, there must be some sort of tool or implement I could use." She thought being pragmatic, and peered around the interior of the building. Her eyes had become accustomed to the darkness of the night, but gradually it had become less so with the arrival of dawn's slow inclusion into the barn, and a pitch-fork that had long ago been tossed carelessly into a corner and was now left rusting on the stone floor, was made visible. Seizing it, Alice hooked the tines of the fork into the locks and with all the effort and strength she could muster kept agitating and forcing them until, they eventually, after much persistence, sprung open. Feeling triumphant, but with sore hands and aching arms, she opened the lid carefully not knowing what would be revealed. "Ugh! I hope it's not a body or anything gruesome," she suddenly thought, but consoled herself immediately at not having smelled rotting flesh. Instead, all she could see were hundreds of small packets securely covered in a plastic filming. "It's drugs! Of course!" She exclaimed with relief. She didn't bother opening the other case as she expected it would hold the same content.

Alice had only ever witnessed this amount of drugs on television newsreels or in films: she was ignorant on whether this haul would be cocaine or heroin? All she now knew was that she would be dispensable once they became tired of her, so she needed to make herself useful to them. But she also needed to be clever and acquire as much knowledge against them for future evidence. So, she began counting the packages on the top layer and then removing some to determine the number of layers and therefore ascertaining the entire content.

Alice's fingers touched against a hard structure in the centre of the case which was unlike any of the other softer parcels. Excited by her find, she carefully pulled it from its concealment and she realised it must be the Klimt sketch she had discovered hidden amongst the drug packets; this was confirmed to her when she opened the crude paper it had been wrapped in. She had to act quickly before anyone came to check on her as the light was brighter now and the new day had begun. Instead of replacing the sketch back inside the case, she hid it under hay bales in another part of the barn, well away from the drugs. She hurriedly closed the lid once all the packages had been replaced exactly how she had found them and with the force of adrenaline coursing through her body and combined with plain determination, she managed to regroup the hay bales as they had been and hoped no one would notice. Lying back down onto her makeshift hay bed, Alice closed her eyes and prayed to God and anyone else who would be listening, that she would soon be delivered safely from this continuing nightmare.

She must have drifted off into a deep sleep through sheer exhaustion because she was violently awakened by something heavy on top of her. Quickly coming to her senses, she alarmingly realised it wasn't a something, but *someone*! She recognised the stomach curdling halitosis of her perpetrator. He was trying to kiss her and she knew that he had probably been drinking vodka most of the night as well and for breakfast. She forcibly tried to push him off her but he grabbed her throat with one hand and wrenched her neck back so that she had difficulty breathing. With his other hand, he succeeded in undoing the zip on his trousers and exposing his penis. She began pounding her fists into his back but without any effect. Instead, he grabbed one of her hands and forced her to hold his erect member, all the time telling her to enjoy and not to struggle or she will die. So, self-preservation got the better of her and she stopped struggling. Laughingly, he leaned over her and with Alice still being forced to hold his penis he forced it into her mouth. Gagging at the foetid smell and taste of it she was made to fellate him, culminating in a climax. Still laughing, he climbed off her and watched her vomiting the contents of her mouth and stomach onto the floor. Distressed and shaking, she was then told she would be 'working' for him and she would be paid in drugs and *kindness* and that had been her first payment in advance.

He then marched her into the farmhouse and ordered her to have a wash as he would need her services later to deliver a special parcel. The matriarch was in the kitchen cooking bacon when she entered and Alice hoped she would empathise with her but all she did was shrug her shoulders when Alice looked pleadingly at her. "Please, I need a drink." She said weakly. The woman turned to pour her a glass of milk and in that moment, Alice saw a knife had been left on the table and grabbed it and slipped it up into her sleeve before anyone had noticed.

Chapter Thirty-One

"We need to find the exact place where Alice's last images were taken from," insisted Emma. "From there, we might be given a clue to her whereabouts *now*." She added firmly. Karl studied the picture that had been taken from the garret and had overlooked the street and fields below.

"We really need to stop and ask someone who looks like they have lived around here for a long time." Karl suggested in reply. "Someone hopefully must recognise the area this was taken from."

They had been headed out of the city and were now on the perimeter where it was becoming more rural; and it felt like they were looking for a needle in the proverbial haystack. The weather had turned miserable to match their moods. The sky had been overcast all day and was becoming darker, when finally, it dispensed a torrent of sleet and hailstones that had been too heavy for it to hold onto any longer. Karl stopped the car as the windscreen wipers had tried furiously in vain to make the road visible and to be able to continue driving. Sitting in the car, they took stock of their surroundings.

"We've been forced to stop here!" Emma suddenly exclaimed. "Something beyond our knowledge, an unknown entity, determined we should find this area." She tried explaining to Karl. "I really do feel we were guided here and were meant to find the exact spot where Alice had been incarcerated *and* I'm getting positive vibes."

Astonished by Emma's sudden outpouring of mystical beliefs, he then looked intently at the buildings and the fields in front of him and compared them with the photograph on the camera. "My God, you're right!" He shouted and gave her a rewarding hug. "Well done, Emma, I knew you were special." And realised he might have overstepped their friendship. He was beginning to have warm feelings towards her, but didn't want to act on them and confuse the complicated situation they were in any further, and had therefore decided to keep it purely platonic, at least for now.

The weather had ceased to be so violent and the sleet had turned into a steady light rain enabling them to see further down the street. They both saw the sign of a café a short distance away and decided they were in urgent need of refreshments. Walking towards it from the car, Emma stopped suddenly and looked back at the corner building they had just passed. A flash of recognition, as if she had been held inside the garret against her will and not Alice, enveloped her, and she knew they would find her friend soon.

They sat inside The Budapest Café as the chairs and tables outside were still dripping wet from the recent downpour. Karl had a slight knowledge of Hungarian and was able to ask the chef for two toasted cheese sandwiches and two cups of coffee which they devoured hungrily. "Can you order another coffee with perhaps a piece of cake this time, while I need to use the loo?" Emma asked Karl as she made her way to the rear of the café.

"Where are the toilets?" She asked the chef in English as she had no knowledge of Hungarian. It was like déjà vu for him, as less than two days ago he had been asked the same thing by another English girl. He must have appeared astonished to Emma, as she then asked him if he was okay. Turning to Karl, who had followed immediately behind her, the chef spoke in Hungarian and explained the similarity and coincidence that had just happened as hardly any English people venture this far out of the centre of the city. Intrigued by this, Karl then asked him to describe, in as much detail as he remembers, the other girl's appearance.

Karl translated everything the chef had told him to Emma after they had sat back down again. He had confirmed that the man in the photo was the same man that had been with the English girl and he had explained how one of his customers had found the camera along with a lipstick written note of *help* and had taken it to the police. They had assumed the police had already acted on this evidence and were dealing with it. Karl laughed at their naivety. Just as the police had done!

Buoyed by this confirmation that they were definitely on the right track, they asked the chef if he knew where the nearest car hire place was. He gave Karl a map of the local area with a list of a few garages that might be possibilities. They decided to try the two nearest ones to where they were, first of all. Both times, they showed the owners the same photo of the man they were looking for, but were met with headshakes and shoulder shrugs. By the third one, they were starting to feel despondent; the garage owner thought he recognised the image he had been shown, but then decided he had been wrong as the man had looked similar to his cousin, he had told them. They had two more to visit. What if neither of them would be helpful? What then? They asked themselves.

The fourth one was in a different neighbourhood and slightly nearer to the city. It was in a built-up area surrounded by many tall apartment blocks that had survived the communist era but were now looking shabby and in need of cosmetic work. The owner, however, was a chubby, clean-shaven older man and relatively smart in his appearance; and paradoxical to his surroundings. He confirmed that he had rented one of his best cars, an Audi, to the gentleman in the photo and the number plate matched the one Karl had partly memorised. He then wanted to know of their interest in locating him. They informed him they were friends of his and had arranged to meet him in Vienna but had unfortunately missed him. And so, without any qualms and smiling, he gave the man's details to them and hoped he had been of help.

Looking on the map they had been given by the chef, they worked out an approximate location. They could see they would need to drive deeper into the countryside to what appeared to be a farmhouse. "Should we wait for the police?" Karl questioned Emma. "No! We'll be wasting time and every minute counts. Besides, they are probably not that far behind us." She replied confidently.

After driving for fifteen minutes, they could see a small herd of cows in a field about a hundred yards ahead of them. Karl slowed the car down on the assumption a farmhouse would be close by. Around the next bend in the lane, they were confronted by a gravel driveway that led to a neglected house with what looked like old abandoned farm machinery left rusting to one side of it. There was a car parked outside but it wasn't the one they were hoping to see. This one was a dirty white colour one with two of its visible hubcaps missing.

"This might not be the farmhouse we're looking for but we should stop and ask anyway." Emma insisted. After knocking on the door, they waited, but no one answered. They peered through a grimy window that had cobwebs in each of its corners, but were unable to see anyone. They knocked again, hoping this time someone would hear. Deciding no one was there, they then walked round the side of the building to see if anyone was at the back of the house or in the vicinity at all. They discovered an older woman dressed all in black tending to a vegetable plot. Startled at hearing foreign voices calling out to her, she dropped the carrots she had been holding. Karl spoke to her kindly in a smattering of Hungarian as he knew she wouldn't know any English. He apologised for frightening her but needed to ask her if she had seen a friend of theirs who had gone missing around here. Emma saw a worried expression cross her face when Karl showed her a photo of Alice, but she had shrugged and shook her head instead. "Are you *sure*?" Emma couldn't help intervening as she had doubted the woman's lack of knowledge.

"Yes, she is sure!" A male voice menacingly replied. Surprised, as they hadn't heard anyone approach them from behind, they both turned to see the same man that has haunted them since seeing his image in Alice's camera. "What do you want?" Again, he sounded threatening and Emma shivered knowing the dreadful person standing three feet away from them had abducted and possibly harmed her best friend.

Chapter Thirty-Two

Alice couldn't wait to scrub her face in the cold water and kept gargling and rinsing her mouth out from the horrific intrusion it had suffered. She was still gagging and heaving at the thought of what had happened to her. A scrappy piece of soap had been left on the filthy, chipped sink which she used to wash under her arms and between her legs to give her some hope of refreshment. A cracked mirror above the sink showed a stranger looking back at her. Horrified at her own gaunt image, the tears began to flow and she became unable to control the sobbing emanating from her suffering, abused body. Despair enveloped her completely until a hammering on the door jolted her and she knew her nightmare was about to continue.

"Hurry up! I need you, come now!" Her perpetrator summonsed. Reluctantly, she emerged from the washroom. He could see she had been crying and said, "Why you cry? I look after you now," and laughed heartily at his good fortune. She still had the knife up her sleeve but knew this wasn't the right time to use it. She will know when! He pulled her through the kitchen and into the yard outside where his car had been parked. "Get in!" He commanded. "We need to do some business and you will be introduced to my *friends*." He pushed her into the front passenger seat and got in beside her. He drove her through the winding country lanes to another remote hamlet containing a handful of old neglected houses; dogs were running and barking outside as the car stopped, supposedly guarding the area and snarling and showing their teeth with effect.

"They won't hurt you; they know me." He reassured her as he pushed her through the menacing beasts and into one of the houses. There were two men inside the smoke-filled room, sitting at a wooden table playing backgammon, who briefly acknowledged their entrance. "This is my new *partner*." He proudly introduced her to them as if she was his chattel. He withdrew a package from his pocket and threw it on the table scattering the dice and counters the men had been playing with. Annoyed by this distraction, they shouted and swore at him.

"This is only part of your order." He said showing indifference to their anger. "My sexy, English girl, here," and with that he pushed Alice forward to stand in front of the table, "will bring the rest, as she is now *working* for me." The two men undressed Alice with their eyes as they scrutinised her body and smirked and nudged each other conspiratorially. Glaring at the idiots salivating in front of her, she knew she had to act very soon and refused to acknowledge them when told to smile.

He pushed her back into the car with force as he was angry with her performance, "You nice to my friends, they pay good money!" He shouted at her. "Tomorrow, you come here!" He threatened, and screeched the tyres as they skidded on the gravel, sending a cloud of dust and stones in the air as the car shot forward. Shaking her head and knowing he was intending to pimp her out to all his cronies, her adrenaline kicked in and in one swift movement she withdrew the knife and stabbed his hand hard until she felt the blade pierce through it completely. He yelled out in pain and disbelief. The car came to a juddering halt as the shock numbed any further movement.

Alice swiftly freed herself from the seat belt, jumped out of the car and ran as fast as she could into the surrounding countryside. She kept close to the hedges and undergrowth so she would be hidden from view. She knew once the shock had worn off, he would come searching for her. This was her one and only chance to be free of him. She had to make it work! Keeping at a parallel to the road but without being seen, she stumbled through stinging nettles and wet grasses; small swarms of midges seem to be following her as if she was wearing a permanent halo. She froze suddenly! A disturbance from behind alerted her, frightened to turn round, a rabbit ran across her path and she almost laughed with relief.

She hoped the knife had pierced a vein and enough damage had been inflicted that he would have to go to get it stitched and bandaged and not bother finding her. But this was wishful thinking, as just as she was hoping this, she heard him angrily shouting abuse and threatening violence against her when he found her. She gauged he was roughly a hundred yards away and would catch her up if she stayed slipping into ditches and tripping over broken branches, so she made a dash for the open lane and hoped a car would come along. She had misjudged the fact that any car travelling on this remote country lane would probably be associated with him. So, when a car slowed down, she realised too late her huge mistake.

"Get in!" A harsh voice commanded. It belonged to one of his 'friends' she had seen earlier. She tried running again but he was faster and stronger and lifted her in a bear hug and carried her to the car. He stopped to collect the other man who scowling at her said she would regret defying him. "No one makes a fool of me!" He stated menacingly. Back at the hamlet, his accomplice pulled her out of the car and lifted her into the open boot of her abductor's car, but this time her hands had been tied together and she had also been gagged.

He drove furiously back through the lanes at a frightening speed; causing Alice to be flung from side to side and banging and bruising her head. He dismissed the many pot holes, as if he was on a purposed built race track and not a slow, uneven country road. He didn't care, he was too angry with her! Let her suffer!

As he approached the farmhouse, he could see an unfamiliar car parked outside. Cautiously, he cut the engine and the car glided to a halt under a group of trees opposite, so as not to be visible from immediate view. Alice sensed there was something wrong as he had stopped cursing at her and had started angrily mumbling; fucking strangers, who here? The last words were barely audible to her but just enough for her to realise they had visitors.

He crept round to the back of the house and saw two foreigners, a man and a woman, questioning his mother. He knew they hadn't heard him arrive as they had been intent on asking the whereabouts of an English girl in the photograph they had been holding.

"What do you want?" He asked aggressively. "I'm her son, talk to me." He saw a fleet of recognition pass in the girl's eyes as they had turned to face him. "Show *me* your photograph." He insisted and Emma had no choice but to hand him the camera. He felt her hand tremble as she handed it to him. "Who is this person? Should I know her?" He exaggerated his questioning as he had begun to enjoy their nervousness and was intrigued at what their next move would be; *I'm the cat and they're the mouses,* he laughingly thought to himself.

"My friend has been missing for two days and the police have informed us that she is in this area." Finding her courage again, Emma stared at him waiting for a reaction. She detected a slight frown and a tightening of his jaw as she spoke these words to him. Karl had let Emma do the talking while he had been studying both the mother's and her son's reactions. He had a hunch they definitely knew something as the mother was staring and pleading with her eyes at her son.

"Sorry, we cannot help you. I hope you find her soon. Goodbye!" Dismissing them, he walked away and went into the farmhouse; with her eyes lowered, the woman followed him carrying her meagre basket of vegetables.

They knew he had been lying to them. Emma's sixth sense was letting her down but she was positive they were in the right vicinity. They walked slowly back to their car that had been parked in front of the house and had expected to see his car there also. "That's strange! How did he arrive then?" They both questioned and looked around for any evidence of a vehicle. Karl suddenly saw a glimpse of chrome shining out from beneath some trees tucked away by the side of the house. Intrigued to see if it was the same car, he had seen speeding past him that night, he went over to investigate further and Emma followed him.

Alice could hear footsteps crunching on the gravel heading towards her and had expected the boot to fly open any second and to be pulled out of her prison. Instead, she recognised both the voices just a breath away. Excitedly, she banged using her tethered hands and kicking with her feet against the metal interior. Stunned by the sudden unexpected noise, Emma called out her name:

"Alice! Alice! Is that you?" A stream of more banging was the reply they had been hoping for.

"Get away from my car *now* or I will shoot you both!" An angry voice informed them as they heard the click of the gun's safety mechanism being released.

Chapter Thirty-Three

They had no doubt that he would pull the trigger on them; he had proved his malevolence when he shot Dominic and had left him for dead. "Please, let Alice out of the boot or she will suffocate!" Emma pleaded with him as she could hear Alice furiously banging about inside it.

"I will release her when I choose to; she still has work for me." He replied alarmingly and with the gun still aimed at them, he marched them into the barn and bolted the door. He was unsure now of what he should do with them. He could kill them but if they weren't bluffing about the police, he would be in serious trouble. Of course, there could be a convenient *accident*; the barn could catch alight or their car could with them inside. With these possibilities formulating in his mind, he was suddenly alerted to the loud sound of police sirens coming his way. He didn't have time to hide their car before two police cars had screeched to a halt next to him. He could see their guns were readily available in holsters should they need to use them. Keep calm, he thought, and just answer their questions.

"What is the matter, officer? Haven't I paid a parking ticket?" He asked trying to be clever and lighten the situation. But he could see it had fallen on deaf ears.

"We need to know your involvement in the disappearance of an English girl two days ago." A policeman from the Viennese police force stated.

"We also have it on good authority that your car was used in the abduction." It was the police from Budapest, who not to feel usurped, informed him.

"That is absurd, this is my car!" He claimed pointing at Karl's car.

Both sets of police were momentarily confounded by this but then realised the number plate was Viennese and not from Budapest. Whilst they were waiting for confirmation on ownership, after phoning the description through to the central bureau, they began to look around.

Alice had heard the sirens and had hoped it was the police, and not an ambulance, and had resumed making as much noise as she was able to. Relieved at hearing the police arrive, Emma and Karl started shouting and causing a commotion from within the barn. When one of the officers started following the sound coming from a car that was just visible amongst the trees, Alice's abductor knew he had to act swiftly. He pulled out his gun and grabbed one of the other officers as a hostage. "I *will* shoot him!" He threatened as he opened the door to Karl's car and forced the officer inside. Still pointing the gun, he got in beside him and turned on the ignition. He was about to drive off when the officer that had investigated Alice's banging, aimed his gun directly at his target; and being qualified as the best marksman in the force, fired his shot and produced a bullseye.

The target slumped over the steering wheel and his blood had been spattered over the officer that had been sitting next to him. For one moment, the officer thought he had been shot and sat stunned. He felt the body next to him for a pulse but he was unable to find one. The mother, appropriately dressed in black, came screaming from the house and became hysterical when she saw her son's lifeless, blood-spattered body. Wailing and beating her chest with her fists, she went limp and collapsed to the ground and had to be carried back into the house and an ambulance was called.

At last, Alice had been released from her nightmare! She was gently lifted out of the car's boot by the crack-shot officer. Traumatised and badly shaken, a blanket had been wrapped around her as she sat inside one of the police vehicles. She couldn't believe her dreadful ordeal was almost at an end.

"Where are my friends?" Alice managed to ask through trembling, parched lips. The police realised the shouts they had heard before the gun had gone off and their actions had been diverted must have emanated from one of the barns. Emma and Karl had been stunned into silence when they had heard the loud gun shot and had prayed that Alice hadn't been on the receiving end. They listened anxiously as approaching footsteps were nearing the barn and half expected to have a gun directed at them. But the police, anticipating their fears, called out to them as they unlocked the door and allowed the sunlight to burst through causing them to blink and become momentarily unfocused. Once they had established that they hadn't been hurt or injured, they were led to where their friend had been taken to recover.

"Alice! Thank God you're okay!" Emma screamed when she saw the dishevelled state she was in. "I got you into this mess, will you ever forgive me?" Hugging her friend tightly and not wanting to let her go for fear of her vanishing again, they sat holding each other while they waited for the ambulance to arrive.

Suddenly, Alice remembered the reason for this entire unfortunate, never to be forgotten adventure; The Klimt Sketch of The Kiss.

"Emma, I hid the sketch in the barn, I hope it's still there." Confused by Alice's sudden declaration, as she hadn't thought about the sketch since her friend had first disappeared, all she could say was "How?" and then "Where?"

Feeling a bit stronger now that she had regained some of her old confidence, she shakily walked arm in arm between Emma and Karl towards the barn. Entering inside again reminded her of the disgusting ordeal that had been inflicted on her by the monster that was now deservedly dead. Sobbing as she relived the trauma in her mind, she wanted to explain to Emma, but couldn't form the words. "Tell me everything you went through when you feel much stronger, I'm here for *you* now!" She said pacifying her with a big hug.

Alice showed them where she had hidden the sketch under the hay bales. It was still there just as she had left it. Emma gently picked it up and wiped off bits of straw and dust powder; a warm glow seeped through her entire being as she unwrapped it, and took a long look at its beauty, she knew then she would be ever grateful to her friend for the sacrifice she had made for its recovery.

Chapter Thirty-Four

The sirens of two ambulances arriving brought the three of them out of the barn. One team of paramedics examined Alice for concussion due to her head injuries and her general weakened appearance; it was decided that Alice would need further treatment and be taken to hospital and possibly have to stay overnight. It was agreed that Emma would travel in the ambulance with her whilst Karl would follow in a police car, as his car was now the scene of a crime and had to be requisitioned.

They had watched as the paramedics removed the dead body from Karl's car; it had been zipped up into a body-bag and carried into the other ambulance. Karl knew he would never want to drive or see that car again. The mother had been so traumatised that she had to be sedated and then wheeled out to ride in the ambulance alongside her dead son.

Alice held Emma's hand all the way to the hospital. She needed the comfort of a lifeline; like an umbilical cord giving sustenance. It had all been worth it despite going through the worse time of her life so far. They were all safe and the sketch had been recovered and above all, she had been reunited with her friends. With this thought in her mind, Alice drifted off into a deep, natural sleep as soon as her head had rested on the hospital pillow.

Now, they knew they could relax as the search was over and Alice was safe, they booked in at a nearby Panziók, a Hungarian bed and breakfast recommended to them by the police; they were told not to go too far as they needed to be available for questioning the following morning. Exhausted and relieved at the outcome, they too welcomed a good night's sleep and were too tired to eat anything. Sharing a room but with separate beds, sleep quickly engulfed them. Should they have had any romantic thoughts, neither had the energy to fulfil them. But now Karl had seen Alice again and she being so vulnerable, he knew his feelings for her had been rekindled and he wanted to help her recovery.

The next morning, they felt reenergised as the watery sun shone through the thin curtains of the boarding house. They were eager to meet the police at the hospital in the hope that Alice was well enough to answer their questions. A taxi arrived to take them as they were unsure how reliable the local transport would be and they were in a hurry to get there. They were told that Alice had had a comfortable night but she was still hooked up to a saline drip as she had lost a lot of body fluids. "How are you feeling?" Emma asked her friend tenderly and gave her a hug, being careful not to disrupt the flow from the tube attached to her hand.

"I need to tell the police everything, it will help me to recover and they need to catch the rest of the gang." She insisted and proceeded to inform them about everything she had witnessed and had experienced. It was heart-breaking for Emma to listen to her dear friend's account and knew she would suffer for quite a while *and* with the possibility of her having post-traumatic stress disorder flashbacks. A mantel of guilt swept over her when she realised the degree of sacrifice Alice had gone through at her behest.

The officer wrote down everything Alice had dictated and then relieved, she signed it to confirm its validity. Due to her detailed description, they were able to arrest the other gang members and recover the stash of drugs from the barn. Apparently, they had known of a group of drug dealers infiltrating their area but had needed to catch the ringleader; which they realised had been Alice's abductor.

Their photo along with Alice's dramatic account of aiding the police to round-up a drug cartel made the next day's headlines on the country's radio and television news channels. They had become famous for the day. A handful of reporters waited patiently outside the hospital's entrance in the hope of getting an interview or at least a photograph. So, when Emma and Karl finally emerged, they were greeted with a tumult of questions and flashlights. And so thankful were the police for all their assistance, they presented Karl with a new car as compensation for having his old one immobilised as evidence.

After spending another night in the hospital, Alice felt strong enough to be discharged and wanted to put as much distance between her and Budapest. She certainly won't be recommending it as a weekend break once back at work! That was the first time, her normal home existence had entered her mind, it seemed like someone else's life, so much had happened to her since then.

"How will I be able to settle down to a dreary mundane life in Northolt again after all this?" She asked Emma.

Chapter Thirty-Five

It was a long drive back to Vienna. The excitement and adrenaline build-up of the last couple of days had depleted their energy store; like an anti-climax after a special event that had been anticipated and planned for a long time. Alice sat quietly in the back of the car thinking of all she had experienced and pondering also the possibilities that could lay ahead for her. She knew her life had definitely reached a crossroad, but was unsure of what direction to take. Karl had been very attentive and caring, but so had Emma, so obviously, it was a friendship love and nothing more. While these thoughts meandered in and out of Alice's mind, Emma had been talking about what she had to do once they were back in Vienna.

"I need to thank Viktor's cousin, Frederik, for his son's assistance in arranging a meeting with the Viennese police and I *must* speak to Viktor himself informing him of the sketch's recovery. He will be thrilled!" She said, excited at the prospect of letting him know his valued artwork is at last safe. "I must also speak to Charles once we know if Dominic is recovering." She said sotto voce, indicating her concern and sympathy for her ex-boss.

Karl had been concentrating driving his smart new vehicle on the busy highway that led them into Vienna. He couldn't believe his luck at being given a new car, especially as he had already thought of replacing the old one; and then he remembered the reason he had been gifted it and felt guilty. The traffic had built up and the queues had become longer as they got nearer to the city. He saw the sign for the ring road which would take them to the hotel they had stayed in previously and aimed for that, assuming they would want to freshen up first.

The hotel welcomed them as if they were heroes. The manager showed them the previous day's newspaper which she had kept as she had recognised their photographs. They were amazed that their notoriety had reached Austria. They were given the best available room at no cost, as she stated it was an honour to have them staying in her humble hotel. She also handed back Alice's suitcase that she had unwillingly abandoned.

"Thank you so much for keeping it safe for me," she said gratefully but surprised. "I need to burn these smelly clothes!" she said pointing at her dishevelled attire.

Karl left them to have their showers and to recuperate and said he would return in a couple of hours as he also needed to go back to his apartment for the same reasons and to make sure his cat was okay; a kind neighbour always fed it if he had to be away, he told them. The two girls hugged and kissed him and thanked him for everything he had been dragged unknowingly into and realised he had become a lifelong friend and not just their taxi driver.

Emma began making those important phone calls once her mobile phone had been recharged. She rang Viktor's cousin, Frederik, first. It was courteous to thank them as without their help, we might not have succeeded, she reminded herself.

"We knew already, we saw you on the news channel, you are heroes!" Frederik exclaimed and invited them to another meal, as a celebration, but this time in a smart restaurant. The next call was to Viktor as she was sure he would be on 'shpilkes'; a Jewish word she had heard Viktor use himself when he was on edge and worried.

"Hannah, it is Emma, is Viktor there?" She asked when Viktor's friend and housekeeper answered the call. "How are you, Emma? We've heard all about how famous you all are from Frederik. I'll just go and get Viktor for you." She replied and went to find him. After a pause of five minutes, Viktor answered. "I am so pleased you are all safe but such risks of your lives for a material object. Nothing is worth that! But I thank you and I shall always remember your kindness and tenaciousness." He said appreciatively but scolding her at the same time. "Now you have the sketch in your possession, would you be able to have it authenticated at The Belvedere Museum before you come home?" He added. "You never did get that far, unfortunately, at The Hadley and I still require it."

"Of course, I will, it will be my pleasure. I shall call them tomorrow for an appointment." She replied, thankful that he still had trust in her. "Goodbye, Viktor, I'll let you know the outcome, hopefully soon." Pleased with how the conversation went, she hung up the call.

Karl had returned by the time she had finished her last call. "I can't believe two hours have gone by so quickly and I still haven't made all the calls I intended to." She said after letting him into the room. Alice had just woken up after a short nap and was pleased to see Karl back with them again. He was aware of the warmth in her eyes when she had looked at him and he hoped he wasn't imagining it as he felt a bond, more than just friendship, forming between them.

"We have all been invited to dine with Frederik and his family tonight at a smart restaurant near to the Opera House." Emma stated while sensing the intimate look between Alice and Karl and making her feel like a spare part. "We shall meet them there, so I hope you know the way, Karl." She added. He nodded without taking his eyes off Alice.

"Instead of phoning the hospital to see how Dominic is, I think we should go there." Emma insisted and hoped they would agree with her change of plan. "I do hope we shall see an improvement in him." She added. So, Karl happily drove them there; he didn't mind as long as he was with Alice, he would go anywhere. He had been thinking that he should be returning to work soon, but as he was self-employed, he had the freedom to choose when and now was definitely not the time. The girls still needed him and he needed to be with Alice!

The neurologist at the hospital took them aside to explain in detail Dominic's condition. He was still being sedated but there had been signs that he was improving slightly; his eyelids flickered in response to having a light shine on them and there had been movement in his hands. "He is still very poorly but we are more concerned about his blood count being very low." He said trying not to alarm them. "This means without a transfusion; he would be susceptible to infection."

"Can you not give him this, then?" Emma asked him.

"We can, but he has been tested and found his blood group to be, B-negative which is rare, and we don't have sufficient resources to be able to proceed." He tried explaining to them. "Has he any relatives with that same blood group that would be able to help him?" The consultant asked.

"I'm not sure but I will phone his brother in England and find out for you." Emma stated trying to sound positive. "But may we see him now?"

Only Emma was allowed into the Intensive Care Unit where Dominic was still being cared for. She was upset to see his position hadn't changed and the numerous tubes, his lifelines, were still in place. Sitting down beside him she held his hand gently; hopefully a comfort for both of them.

"It's me, Emma," she whispered close to his ear. "Please get better, I know things went wrong but we are all worried now and you need to get stronger." She detected a slight grip of his hand as she was speaking to him. "Thank God! I think you can hear me, am I right?" His hand gripped hers again. Excited, she buzzed for a nurse and explained what had happened. The neurologist came and looked into Dominic's eyes and could see the pupils were dilated. "It seems you have stimulated a reaction in him, I'm pleased to say. Well done! But he needs to be quiet now and we will look in on him again soon." Before showing them out of the ward, Emma again said she would speak to his family and then let him know the outcome. They shook hands and thanked him for all their care and kindness.

Alice and Karl had waited in the family room for Emma to return. He had had his arm around Alice's shoulders but quickly removed it when Emma had walked in. "You don't have to look so guilty; I know what's happening, I have eyes!" She laughed at them but relieved to have seen a positive improvement in Dominic. As they got back into the car, she told them she needed to get back to the hotel so that she could make a private call to Charles. She knew it would be difficult for him and hoped he wouldn't blame her for his brother's present, dreadful condition.

Emma called Charles on The Hadley Gallery number as she didn't have his personal mobile phone details. It rang a few times before being answered.

Chapter Thirty-Six

It was Helena who had picked up the receiver. "Helena, it is Emma here, I need to speak to your father urgently." She said firmly. But Helena was intrigued as to why Emma should be calling and wasn't ready to hand the call over.

"What do you want? I thought we'd got rid of you!" The other girl replied nastily. "I'm not sure where my father is right now." She added playing for time.

"Helena, don't be a prat! This is about your uncle Dominic, it's important. He is in *hospital*!" She stressed to make the girl realise she needed to stop the feuding and get Charles to the phone.

"Hang on then," she said, already bored with the conversation and not even bothering to ask the reason why her uncle would be in hospital.

Charles had been completing a sale with a new client and was annoyed at being called to the phone. "Tell them to call back as I am busy." He said sharply to Helena as he continued to fawn over the perfect choice his client had just made; a ceramic bowl that had been gathering dust and thankfully he had finally sold.

"Ok, but it's Emma, something about Uncle Dominic being in hospital." She said without showing any concern.

Charles expedited the meeting and hurried to the phone in his office. "Emma, what has happened? Where's Dominic? Is he okay?" The questions poured out of him before Emma had a chance to answer.

She quickly informed him of Dominic's slight improvement as she needed to calm him down before telling him the whole story. The call lasted a full hour as he needed to know of his brother's duplicitous actions that had led to her friend, Alice, being kidnapped.

"I'm sorry I didn't inform you immediately after he had been shot but Alice had been my main concern and I was angry at Dominic for the way he had cheated everybody, including you." She stated, once she had finished explaining everything to him plus the fact that he had initially stolen the sketch and had framed her for it. She omitted to tell him that she also had a strong inkling that Helena had been an accomplice and had stolen it at Dominic's behest, but thought better of it as Charles had already had a surplus of shocking information to register and she didn't want him to counter her theory.

Charles was stupefied to learn of his brother's nefarious dealings and horrified that Emma had been dismissed to cover them up. He apologised profusely and immediately said she would be reinstated whenever she was ready, that's if she was agreeable to working back at the gallery again. She thanked him, but felt unsure, as she had been extremely hurt by their accusations and said she would have to decide at a later date when she wasn't so confused by all that has happened in such a short space of time.

"Charles, the hospital has stressed that Dominic is in urgent need of a blood transfusion for him to be able to recover. As his blood group is rare, they wondered if a family member might share the same B-negative blood group." She informed him and making him aware of the urgent situation he was now in.

"I'm not sure if I *am* a match as my blood group is O Positive, but as a long shot, I will find out what Helena's is. I will ask Sadie also and let you know. Regardless of whether any of us are a match, I wish to fly out to see him and speak to the doctors myself." He added, as he didn't want Emma shouldering the burden of making important life changing decisions on behalf of his brother. Before ending the call, Emma gave Charles the hospital's details as he wanted to call them immediately, and told her he will also be booking a flight out for the next day.

Unnerved by the news of Dominic's serious condition and the fact that his brother had lied to him all along, Charles decided to close the gallery. He felt unable to concentrate on his normal working routine or focus on irrelevant matters when his brother's life was at stake; regardless of his wrongdoings, he was still his only living blood relative. The only other time the gallery ever gets closed is on Christmas Day each year. He also cancelled two meetings he had previously booked for the next day and pushed them back to the following week; in the hope that Dominic's situation would have improved and normality would be resumed. Helena was filing her nails when he found her in Emma's former office in the basement. Alerted to his descending footsteps, she had quickly picked up the nearest book and had pretended to be copying information from it.

"Too late, Helena, I don't know why you are still on the payroll as you continue to show little interest in being here, never mind actually working." He admonished, realising she would never become a reliable member of the team. "I am closing the gallery for today and probably for the coming week." He informed her. "So, collect your belongings as we are going home now." She knew things must be serious with her uncle as the gallery never gets closed for more than a day. Still, that would suit her; she'll be able to languish in bed in the morning. Not to aggravate her father any more, she gathered up her things and was out of the door and in the car park before Charles had even set the alarms and locked the main door.

Sadie was surprised when she heard Charles' car turn into the driveway and rushed to open the front door. "Uncle Dominic's in hospital." Helena threw out as an explanation when she saw her mother's eyebrows raised in puzzlement; like two inverted commas. Charles explained in detail the full conversation he had had with Emma earlier. Distressed at hearing that Dominic required a blood transfusion to keep him alive and that the hospital in Vienna had asked for any of his relatives to come forward that had a possible matching blood group, Sadie's face visibly started to ashen in front of Charles.

"I'm going to book for the three of us to fly out to Vienna tomorrow and not waste any more time. My brother is in desperate need of our blood to save his life and they can test us all when we get there. I will ring the hospital to let them know we will be coming." Positive that he had made the right decision, Charles booked three plane tickets to arrive in Vienna the following morning.

Sadie knew she had no say in the matter and it would be useless to try to persuade Charles to have her remain at home. But she knew her future would depend on the outcome of this trip and whether he would ultimately forgive her.

Chapter Thirty-Seven

The three of them met Frederik and his family outside The Opera House in the heart of Vienna's popular tourist sector, but being winter, the tourists were still thin on the ground; there were just a few more weeks before they would return to enjoy the Christmas festivities. Its ornate architecture was emphasised by the light from the curved lamps on all sides highlighting the unmistakable magnificence of the building. It was only a short walk away to the restaurant but Emma and Alice wanted to feel carefree as if they were on holiday and try to dismiss, for one night, all that had occurred in the last week. They were all there dressed in their finery; Frederik and his wife, Frederik's son, Joseph and his stylish wife and their two children, both girls dressed alike in faux fur pink coats. They were greeted with much hugging and cheek kissing as the obvious relief of seeing them all safe was a joy.

The heart-warming sound of an orchestra playing escaped each time a door to the renowned concert house was opened; and Emma knew that the fortunate audience inside would be enjoying an evening of magical music and singing. It all added to the convivial atmosphere of being with such a kind and welcoming family, all talking and laughing together. The restaurant was in fact opposite, and only across the road. Even in winter, there were horses and carriages, called fiakers, taking visitors wrapped in cloaks and blankets on romantic sight-seeing rides around the city. They waited and waved at the occupants as they went by before crossing the road and into the warmth of the restaurant.

Once inside, they were all escorted by the maître d' towards a warmly heated glass conservatory; it had been bedecked with seasonal flower arrangements and led off from the main dining area. As they were a large group and required the additional space, Frederik had requested this in advance to ensure they would enjoy this private facility which would add to their unrestricted merriment of the evening ahead. Emma felt privileged to be amongst such a generous and openly affectionate family, so unlike anything she had ever experienced back in her provincial home town of Ruislip or even in London. This is her calling; this is where she belongs; amidst the culture of music and art appreciation as if she had returned to a life she had previously led. Lost in her own glorious reverie, she hadn't realised Karl had stood up with a glass of champagne in his hand and was clinking the side of it with a spoon waiting to be heard. It had produced the right effect and the table instantly became silent.

"First of all, I would like to thank everyone sitting around this beautifully laid table, enjoying a delicious meal and in such a grand setting, to raise their glasses and drink a toast to being safe, happy and alive." He announced, and took a sip from his glass. "L'Chaim! L'Chaim!" They all shouted together as they raised their own glasses. "To Life!" Emma and Alice both agreed, guessing correctly their sentiment. "Whilst I am still standing and not to waste the champagne, I would also like to express my growing love for a certain lady here with me tonight. She has been very brave and has suffered extremely, but now I would like to ask her to stay with me in Vienna so that I can make sure she will always be safe." Karl turned to Alice who had been sitting next to him and waited for her reply. Stunned by Karl's unexpected speech, Alice jumped up and hugging him exclaimed "Of course, I will, I love you too." The resounding noise of clapping brought the waiters running as if the restaurant had been struck by thunder and lightning. With everyone talking at once, it was difficult to hear herself speak, but Emma knew she had to put her reservations aside and be pleased for her friend. And so, she stood up to reply to Karl's toast, "I hope Karl will always be there for you even though you haven't known each other for very long. Be happy, you deserve it." She said looking intently at Alice and raising her glass in salutation. She would miss her loyal friendship but knew she couldn't stand in her way of happiness. "Hear! Hear!" The chorus of their new friends agreed and clapped their hands in appreciation of the perfect ending to a perfect evening.

The dinner was a total success; it had instilled in Emma the importance of surrounding yourself with the right people, ones who are trusting and caring and she didn't blame Alice at all for wanting to remain amongst them. Once outside and sated from an evening of fine food and wine, they stood chatting and expressing their goodbyes in unison. Karl hailed a passing fiaker that had just deposited a couple at a café further down the road; the driver was pleased to have another fare and quickly pulled on the reins and the horses stopped immediately next to them.

"I hope you don't mind, Emma, if I take Alice along for a ride alone as it's such a lovely crisp, clear night?" He asked. "No, go ahead, please, I'll take a taxi back to the hotel." She replied, feeling slightly envious of her friend's sudden romance. The others all cheered as Karl helped Alice up into the carriage and lovingly wrapped the available fur rug around her legs for warmth and then watched as the horses trotted off into the starry night; with the sound of their hooves echoing on the cobblestones, and a cloud of their vaporised air lingering long after they had turned the corner.

"Don't worry, Emma, we'll take you back to your hotel," Joseph informed her. "We would not dream of you getting a taxi on your own." He added reassuring her further. "Thank you so much, that is very kind of you." She replied grateful of their hospitality towards her and making her feel less alone. Since Karl and Alice had declared their love for each other, that is exactly the feeling that had swept over her, one of loneliness; her friend deserting her, like a child losing its favourite teddy bear. Emptiness!

She was just in the throes of falling asleep when Alice tiptoed into their hotel room. "I'm sorry if I've woken you," she said softly as Emma struggled to open her eyes and focus. "Karl has asked me to marry him and I've accepted!" Alice in her excitement bounced on Emma's bed causing the bedside clock to fall onto the floor and release the alarm mechanism. The high-pitched ringing lasted a few seconds before they could find the light to be able to see to turn it off.

"Now, you've woken the whole hotel up; we will be thrown out." Emma said seriously and then started laughing uncontrollably with delight for Alice.

The following morning, Emma arranged for a taxi to take her to The Belvedere to have the sketch authenticated before meeting up with Charles later on in the day. She would have phoned them first, but decided to pre-empt any situation where she might be fobbed off with a lame excuse as for her not to go there in person. She had carefully locked it in the room's safe and had checked on it regularly to ensure its safety. Alice and Karl were out sightseeing for the day as he wanted to impress her with his home city's finest attractions. Karl had asked Emma if she would like to go with them, but she knew she couldn't accept his invitation as they had wanted to have time alone, but had thanked him anyway for his thoughtfulness.

The taxi had dropped her off outside an ordinary looking building; nothing like what she had expected at all, but that impression was soon to change. With the sketch held tightly under her arm, Emma had been directed through the reception area and into a courtyard. She had been told to go to the Upper Belvedere where she would be met by one of the curators who will be waiting for her at the entrance. Walking out into the late November sunshine, she was thankful that the sky was a clear, wintry blue and without any hint of a grey cloud in sight. The view that greeted her took her breath away, "My word!" she exclaimed openly and not caring if anyone had heard her. "This is amazing!" In front of her stretched, what seemed like a half mile, of beautifully landscaped gardens complete with water fountains and rising gently to a hill with the Belvedere Museum at its summit; a Majesty surveying all the land below. It proved a long walk to the top as the higher she became, Emma kept stopping to take in the view of the city starting to unfold in the distance.

Finally, she reached the portal where a young woman had been waiting for her and had obviously been watching her progress. "Wonderful view, and well worth the climb!" The woman stated as she held out her hand for Emma to shake. "Please to meet you, Miss Fogle, my name is Lydia. I'm head of collections." Emma, momentarily lost for words nervously replied, "Please, call me Emma." She followed Lydia into a large ground-floor office where other members of her team were busy working but had looked up curiously, when they had entered. "I believe you have brought me something to study and authenticate for you, have you not?" She questioned Emma. Placing the sketch onto a bench, Emma briefly explained to Lydia its provenance and the reason she had it in her possession. "I won't be able to give you a result today, I'm afraid. Will you be able to leave it here with me for a day or so?"

"Of course, I hadn't expected you to be able to tell me immediately as I'm sure you are very busy and I have arrived unexpectedly." Emma replied as she carefully uncovered the sketch and then stood back in expectation. A surprised expression fleetingly crossed Lydia's face as if a butterfly had flown pass. "Is there something wrong?" Emma asked.

"No, I'm not sure, but I will be able to confirm its authenticity once I and my team have studied it further, please rest assured." The young woman kindly smiled and walked with Emma back the way she had come. Going back down the hill didn't take as long, as she had been confused by Lydia's puzzled demeanour and this time, deep in thought, hadn't noticed the beauty of her surroundings. She felt her pocket vibrate and realised her mobile phone was alerting her attention. "Hello?"

"Emma, it's Charles, we've just landed. Can we meet you at the hospital this afternoon, about 2 pm, if that's all right with you?"

"Not a problem, Charles. I'll see you there."

Chapter Thirty-Eight

It was very strange for Emma to see Charles again, especially under these harrowing circumstances. She had revered him as her boss, but after the way he had believed she could ever had been untrustworthy, she realised the hurt was still evident. She knew she would have to move forward and try to forgive him or it will ruin her future. "Do I want a future with The Hadley?" she asked herself. "Should I risk being there again?" She *had* been thinking about it since Charles had mentioned it to her, but she was still undecided. "It would have to be on my terms!" was her last thought before being introduced to his wife, Sadie, who had extended a perfectly manicured hand towards her as a greeting. Tall, elegant and impeccably dressed, Emma could see the connection between Charles and her; they were definitely a well-matched couple. How on earth Helena came into the equation, she did not know, except that she knew they had come as a package and Charles had gallantly taken on the small parcel.

Emma introduced the new arrivals to Dominic's consultant who suggested that they should have their blood tests done immediately, before taking them to see Dominic. One by one, they followed a nurse into a side room. Helena, true to form, reluctantly questioned the necessity of having her blood taken and began making excuses for it not to happen; they ranged from her having an adverse reaction to needles to being anaemic and fainting, and they wouldn't want that on their conscience, she had told them emphatically.

Regardless, they all had it done and then they were taken to see Dominic who was still in the Intensive Care Unit. As they were family, two were allowed in together and so Charles took Helena in with him first of all. The smell of the disinfectant, the humming of the machinery and the imagery of his brother's helpless, impotent body assaulted Charles' senses and he wanted to vomit. He had always kept his feelings under tight control, but now wasn't the time for having a regimented, stiff upper lip; his brother needed him and so he went to sit beside him and cautiously reached out to hold his hand. "I am here now,

Dominic. It's your brother, Charles." Helena stood behind him unsure of what she should say or do. To her, it seemed like an imposter was laying there and not the arrogant man she knew that was her uncle. Nothing affected *that* man; who was strong, suave and capable of anything he put his mind to, not *this* person a weak replica, an ersatz copy, a counterfeit. Not him! Shocked at her own strong emotions, Helena ran outside crying uncontrollably.

"What if he dies?" She pleadingly asked Sadie in between her sobbing. "We won't let him! Once he has had a taste of one of our blood samples, he'll be like Dracula rising from a deep sleep with a renewed strength." Sadie said, trying to make her smile and lighten the mood. "If you are feeling a bit better, I'm going to join your father while you stay here with Emma."

Emma had just witnessed a different, softer side to Helena; she had been almost childlike in asking for her mother's affirmation to help ease her sadness, like kissing her knee after grazing it from a fall. "Is there any chance we can stop being enemies?" Emma asked Helena as she went to sit down in the chair opposite her. "I was never a threat to you, Helena, I promise; it was all in your mind. We could even have been friends." Helena weighed up this statement Emma had just declared in her mind carefully before giving her answer; was it worth carrying on a feud when potentially Emma had done nothing but innocently join the gallery's workforce, whereas she had been a jealous bitch from the start and contrived in getting her sacked. Plus, she might also be useful to her one day as Uncle Dominic used to tell her *not* to burn her bridges.

"Perhaps, you are right." She eventually replied coming to a conclusion. "I've not been helpful or friendly to you. Let's forget about the past and start again." They both smiled tentatively and both not entirely convinced that that will happen.

Sadie joined her husband at Dominic's bedside and could see why Helena had been so distraught. A vision flickered into her psyche, like a re-run of old home movies, of the last time she had seen Dominic. It had been at their garden barbeque when he had looked so tanned and handsome, a model of a gentleman except she knew he had never been a gentleman; a ladies' man, yes!

The doctor arrived authoritatively armed with a folder containing Dominic's notes and ready for any questions Charles had wanted to ask him. He explained that Dominic required a full blood transfusion as soon as possible and that they would have the results of their blood tests within the hour. "Each day, there have been slow signs of improvement which is an indication that he has the spirit to fight and not give in." He gave them this snippet of information to boost their morale as he could see they needed the encouragement to keep positive. "Whilst we are analysing your blood samples, would you also be in agreement for us to compare your DNA in case we will require further surgery, such as stem cell?" He asked Charles expecting their full co-operation. Charles took the doctor aside as he had wanted to confidentially explain to him, without Helena hearing, that she wasn't his biological daughter but he had adopted her when she was very young.

"Thank you for making us aware of that fact, otherwise it could have been confusing for us and embarrassing for you." He smiled, and left them to get a much-needed coffee each and then to sit and wait for the test results.

Emma sat apart from Charles and his family as she wasn't in the mood for making small talk. She had only just been introduced to Sadie and didn't feel that it was the right time for further generalised conversations. Anyway, she had noticed how her demeanour had changed from seeming outwardly poised to one of nervousness after the doctor had spoken to them. It had been a subtle transition, but Emma recognised the tell-tale signs; her hand shaking as she held the coffee cup, the re-crossing and uncrossing of her legs and the biting of her bottom lip continually so that she needed to reapply her lipstick and keep occupied. *All is not as it seems in that family,* she thought to herself. "My instinct tells me it involves Dominic, it usually does!"

They all stood up when they saw the doctor walking towards them; all except Helena who had been deep in conversation on her mobile phone with a friend from home, and whining that she would rather be there than stuck in some smelly hospital. "Finish the call, Helena, you're being rude!" Charles said disapproving of his daughter's behaviour and apologised to the doctor.

"Would you all like to sit down as I need to impart to you the information we have discovered through our testing." They all sat down. Charles with his fingers metaphorically crossed, Sadie with hers visibly trembling and Helena with hers in her mouth biting her nails. "Well, this has been most interesting," he went on to explain. "First of all, we have a good blood match that would be suitable for a transfusion to give to your brother," and he directed his gaze to Charles. "Helena would be a perfect donor as not only is her blood a suitable match but we have discovered that her DNA matches Dominic's completely." Hearing her name mentioned brought Helena out of her indifference and for once, she became dumbfounded. Ironically, the blood drained from Sadie's face and she began to shake uncontrollably, knowing that her husband would very soon realise the meaning of the information that they had just been given. Emma looked at Charles and she was aware of the exact moment the proverbial penny had dropped. His anger rose from deep within him and exploded with great force, like a volcano spitting out molten lava, but this was hot venom pouring out of him.

"How could you? You bitch!" He shouted at Sadie forgetting where they were. "You have tricked and deceived me all these years *and* with my own *brother*! I can never forgive you!" He bellowed and stormed out of the hospital. Shocked by the scene that had just unfolded in front of her, Emma apologised profusely to the doctor and suggested they should all go outside for some much-needed fresh air.

"Hopefully, they will be back soon once the anger has subsided and a decision can be made to proceed with Dominic's treatment." She said, hoping this would be the case.

Charles was nowhere to be seen and Sadie was consoling Helena by stroking her hair as if she was a puppy dog. Emma could see that they were both in a state of limbo with Sadie trying to placate her daughter with hugs and words of love. But Helena wasn't that easy to be placated, "So, now I've got to call Uncle Dominic, *Father*, that's gross!" Poor Sadie, with her secret out at last, she had no allies.

Chapter Thirty-Nine

The Hadley Family had temporarily disbanded; Charles was nowhere to be found and Sadie had clung to Helena for support hoping for forgiveness from her contrary daughter. They were huddled together for warmth on a bench in the hospital gardens as they had hurriedly abandoned their coats inside when they had run after Charles. Emma had never felt so impotent; should she commiserate or comfort them? But she felt it wasn't really her place to become involved as she didn't know them well enough. Instead, she decided to find where the cafeteria was inside the hospital and wait for them to return, which by the look of the sky it shouldn't be too long. Any minute now, the heavens will open as the dark rain clouds had been threatening all day, and if they don't come inside soon, they will all get drenched.

She was sipping at her much-welcomed hot chocolate and wondering how Alice was, when her phone rang. "You must be psychic; I was just thinking about you." She exclaimed, pleased to hear from her friend and having a good reason to talk about something else other than blood tests. Although she did briefly divulge the latest hot news about 'The Hadley's'' to her. "Nothing is ever straight forward in your world, is it Emma?" Alice replied, thankful that now she had a wonderful future ahead of her and a chance to be settled.

"Listen, Emma, I'm calling to let you know that Karl is taking me to visit his parents in Bratislava for a few days, so you'll have the room all to yourself." She said laughing and sounding very happy.

"Where is that?" She asked feeling slightly disgruntled at being left alone. "It sounds a long way!"

"No, it's only an hour away in the car, so don't worry, I'll be back soon and we can all go out for a meal to celebrate, just the three of us this time." She added, said goodbye and hung up; leaving Emma downhearted with nothing but aggravation and other people's problems in her immediate future. The hot chocolate had been delicious and she was contemplating ordering another when she saw Sadie and Helena enter the cafeteria. "Has Charles returned?" Emma asked them.

"We have been looking for him and thought he might be here, but obviously not." Sadie replied looking round the sparsely occupied room. "It's pouring down outside, so I expect he'll turn up soon." Emma ordered three more hot chocolates to help warm their spirits as well as their bodies. "I don't wish to pry, but will you still go ahead with Helena giving blood?" Emma asked Sadie who had been stirring her hot drink continually and staring aimlessly as the bubbles collected in the centre like a small eddy.

"Yes, Helena has agreed to help Dominic despite the traumatic revelations she has had to witness today which is very commendable. Don't you think?" She said, smiling encouragingly at her daughter, who for once hadn't complained.

"Then perhaps, maybe we should make our way upstairs as I'm sure the doctor will be waiting for guidance as whether the transfusion is to continue." They both agreed and followed Emma to the stairs. They were shocked to see Charles deep in conversation with the consultant. He ignored Sadie completely and informed Helena that the hospital feels it would be better for her to be admitted for one night as she might feel very weak afterwards.

"I'll do it if you make it worth my while." Helena condescendingly stated to Charles. "Surely, I will deserve a reward afterwards!" Furious at her selfishness, Charles for the first time looked at her with renewed eyes, "It all makes sense now. I often wondered where you got your devious streak from and now, I know. You and your *uncle* are like two peas in a pod. I even noticed you both have a similar birthmark on your upper right arms." He seemed unable to stop, it was as if he was being purged and the floodgates had finally opened. Turning to Sadie, and not in the least embarrassed that the doctor was still amongst them, "She's your daughter, your love child, you deal with her and you can accept her bribery if you wish to! You stay with her and I will go to the hotel and collect her things for an overnight stay." And all in the same breath, he asked if Emma would go with him. Relieved to be getting away from the toxic atmosphere that was becoming embarrassing for her, she agreed to accompany him. After apologising profusely to her, they sat in silence until they reached the hotel. She could see that he was still fuming and muttering to himself as he left her waiting in the car while he went inside. "I won't be long." He managed to say before he was out of earshot.

His mood seemed to have improved on their return journey back to the hospital. Emma was bewildered and wondered why he had wanted her to be with him as he hadn't said much to her other than to keep apologising. So, she decided to tell him about the sketch and to help turn his mind back to something he was experienced in, the subject of art. She had already informed him that it was back in her possession but he wasn't aware that Viktor Bloom had asked her to take it to The Belvedere for authentication. "Of course, he would, we had made such a hash of it when *we* had the chance!" He interjected, and then allowed her to continue. She told him of her misgivings after she had left it there that morning and the puzzled expression that had briefly shown on the woman's face as it had been unwrapped.

"Wait until she calls you and if you would like me to go with you, I would be only too pleased to offer you my professional support. But first of all, let me take you back to your hotel or wherever you wish to be as I'm sure you have had enough of my family for one day, I know I certainly have. I will call you tomorrow and make you aware of the status quo regarding the transfusion." He smiled and at last, looked more able to contemplate the task ahead of him regarding the direction his family would take.

Chapter Forty

Karl was proud to introduce Alice as his fiancée to his parents. He had previously described her to them over the phone and they had been impatient to meet her in person. At last, their only, beloved son had found someone to settle down with and they hoped she would be suitable and not a 'hippie' like one of his other girlfriends was; to them, this was anyone who dressed unconventionally and with long flowing hair and talked of saving the planet. They weren't disappointed and they hugged and welcomed Alice as soon as she had been introduced to them. They didn't speak any English and Karl had to interpret for her their approval at their son's choice, making Alice feel as if she could be returned to the shop if they had found the goods to be faulty or not to their liking. They lived in a small bungalow outside of the city centre. Karl explained that they used to live in one of the high-rise apartments; a concrete jungle, that had originally been built for the workers during the communist era, and it still stands as the largest development of the former Eastern Bloc. But now they were content as they had a garden to grow vegetables in and could sit and relax in fresh, clean air.

That evening Karl was eager to show Alice the stunning view from the famous castle that dominated high up on a hill and overlooked the old town of Bratislava. He had often visited it on his own and always felt envious watching people being able to share such a wonderful panoramic view with their loved ones. He had forewarned Alice that she would need to wear flat shoes as there would be many steps to climb and quite a bit of walking.

"Have we nearly reached the top yet?" Alice asked hopefully, in between catching her breath. "You were right to warn me but I didn't realise there would be quite so many."

"You will see, it'll be worth it." He promised and took hold of her hand to encourage her to carry on. It was quite windy when they reached the top, and the sky was just turning from dusk to an indigo blue that still retained a hint of a pink streak from a faded setting sun when they finally walked out onto the concourse in front of the castle. They were told they would have to be quick as the castle gates were about to close.

"So, you dragged me up here and we can't even stay to see anything!" Alice exclaimed wanting to sit down after the exertion of the long ascent. "Remind me never to climb Everest." She added pathetically, knowing she was being dramatic.

"Come, look!" Karl ignored her and pulled her over to the surrounding wall. She hadn't the strength to refuse him and allowed herself to be led. The view before her took the remainder of her breath away as there was so much to see. In the far distance, she could just see Austria, where they had travelled from that morning. Hungary was also barely visible before it became completely dark. But looking down, she could see the River Danube lit up along its banks; it looked so sleek as if it had just been painted in oils.

"It is truly beautiful, now I know why Strauss had been so impressed by it." She laughed and began humming the first bars to the infamous 'Blue Danube Waltz'.

"Sorry, but we have to go now; perhaps, I should have waited to bring you here in daylight. I was too eager to show you my favourite place." The descent was less strenuous but more hazardous as the enveloping darkness meant they had to tread slowly even though there were small spotlights along the way which helped to guide them. They gave a sigh of relief as they reached the bottom and the view, Alice thought, was even more stunning, but she wouldn't tell Karl that.

"It's so romantic, Karl, with the boats on the river lit up as well as the bridge in the distance, and the stars outdoing all the artificial lighting with their own brilliant sparkling display. Thank you for bringing me here!" She pulled him towards her and put both her arms around his neck and treated him to a long, passionate kiss. "Now, let us go back to our hotel where I can continue thanking you." She said cheekily.

"I'm so glad my parents do not have a spare room." He added and chuckled.

Despite her longing to be fully intimate with him, Alice froze as soon as Karl went to touch her. Even though they were unofficially engaged, she had wanted for them to get to know each other more and for it not to be just about sex. They had showered on their return and were now lying naked in bed together; she had envisaged their first love-making to be ardent and arousing but also gentle and loving. Instead, surprisingly she had flinched and pushed him away.

"I'm so sorry I don't know why that happened." She apologised, but embarrassed at her unexpected rejection of his love.

"I do." He said caringly. "You have been through so much and have not given yourself the time to cleanse your mind of the horrifying experiences you have had to deal with." She pondered thoughtfully at Karl's accurate analysis of her reaction and realised he had been spot-on. She had been suffering flashbacks in her dreams at night and each time, she saw the distorted face of that dreadful man, her abductor, looming over her, she awoke in a sweat and had heard herself shout out, 'No!'

"You're right, Karl, but how am I ever going to forget?" She started crying uncontrollably and he took her gently in his arms and cradled her like a baby. "You will, I will help you, I promise." She remained enveloped in his arms throughout the night and felt comforted by the warmth and musky smell of his body and for the first time since her assault she had had a peaceful, trouble-free sleep.

They spent the majority of the following day with his parents before making their excuses and heading back to Vienna; they felt they selfishly needed to be alone and it had been a strain on Alice to maintain a permanent smile when she didn't understand the discussions Karl was having between his parents, which ultimately made her feel a complete outsider. Besides, she knew Emma would require her support against 'the Hadleys', even if it was only a moral one, just to help balance the scales.

As they drove out of Bratislava, Alice could see the castle on the hill following them to their right-hand side; blatantly standing out, a magnificent white cube against the grey November sky and with its brown turrets pointing heavenward as if bidding them a safe journey and a fond farewell.

Chapter Forty-One

Helena had been left weakened by the transfusion and the insistence of the hospital for her to recover in one of their side wards had been essential, as she had needed time to replace the several pints of blood that had been extracted from her. Sadie had stayed the night in the hospital, although she knew Helena would be in safe hands, it was an excuse not to face Charles' recriminations. She had slept fitfully in the relative's room across three padded-vinyl chairs with her coat rolled for a pillow and had woken with a stiff neck and pins and needles cramping one of her legs. Blurry eyed, she hadn't dared to look in a mirror as she knew her mascara would have smudged resulting in 'Panda' eyes. Her main aim now was to find a washroom before anyone saw her looking so dishevelled; the alter ego to the poised, immaculate woman of the previous day.

Charles had decided to try to obliterate his problems by drowning them in a succession of the city's bars. Indeed, he had been so successful after matching shot for shot of slivovic (plum brandy) with a native, but had finally conceded after he had been ill in the men's toilets and had wanted to lie down. Fortunately, he had a smattering of self-respect left in him just enough to call a taxi back to his hotel. So unknowingly, he had also woken the next morning with blurry eyes and a stiff neck, but with the added mandatory splitting headache. After downing two full glasses of water and a mug of strong, hot coffee, he had felt more like facing the aggravation of the day ahead. "When did I become so negative?" He mumbled to himself. He knew he shouldn't drive to the hospital. There was still too much alcohol in his system and the thought of spending the day in an Austrian cell to sober up prompted him to call a trusty cab.

And so, when they appeared at the reception desk and both looking the worst for wear and glaring at each other and had asked to see their daughter, the hospital receptionist apologised for not recognising them and had immediately offered to fetch them some more caffeine to help boost their urgent daily intake. They gratefully accepted the corrugated cardboard cups containing the coffee; a similar design in the grey, colour and texture of other receptacles used generally in hospitals for more personal matters. But the coffee had tasted good and had been just what they had needed.

Seeing Helena looking as pale as the sheet that was covering her it brought both their parental instincts to the fore. Despite discovering she was his brother's child; he had raised her to the best of his ability always knowing she hadn't biologically been his. He still loved her, even though she could be difficult and strong-willed, a trait he had once admired in her as he had hoped she would one day head the gallery. But now, for the first time, he had reservations about the future.

"We do need to talk properly, Charles. I need to explain certain things to you. Please!" Sadie talking to him brought him out of his reverie with a jolt.

"I'll listen but not here and not now!" He replied emphatically. Helena had been aware that her parents were there but had not wanted to open her eyes until that moment, trying hard to pretend things were as they used to be before all the arguments. "Please don't start arguing again, I'm too tired to have you both bickering over me." She feebly pleaded with them.

Just then, the doctor entered the room and greeted them with a smile, which they took to be a positive sign that all had gone well.

"You will be pleased to know that the blood transfusion has been a success and Dominic is already showing immediate signs of improvement. I am sure you would like to see him?" He said raising one eyebrow to emphasise this was a question in case he had read their moods incorrectly.

"You go, Charles, while I'll stay here with Helena as I don't wish to cause you any further discomfort in front of your brother." Sadie said worried that she might be witness to a confrontation between them which seemed to be inevitable. So, Charles left Sadie to help Helena get ready as she seemed well enough to be discharged from hospital that morning. Charles cautiously opened the door to Dominic's room expecting to see his brother as he had last seen him; surrounded by a plethora of tubes attached to pulsating machines making intermittent bleeping sounds. But now, only one tube remained, the one to monitor his heartbeat. Dominic had been brought out of his enforced coma the night before, once the doctors knew the transfusion had been a success. Although the damage he had sustained to his head when he had fallen, had brought on a mild stroke. The doctor had pre-warned Charles that hopefully in time, Dominic's slurred speech and his inability to lift his right arm should improve with the aid of

156

therapy. The door opening had shifted the air in the room and Dominic slowly opened his eyes to see what had been the cause of the displacement. He had to blink several times before believing that it was his brother Charles standing in the doorway. Tears automatically started rolling down his face at the relief of seeing him there. He tried to speak but his tongue felt heavy as if it had been glued down.

"Don't try to talk." Charles advised him. "I'll do the talking and you just need to listen." He then proceeded to refresh his brother's memory as to the reason he had been admitted into the hospital in case his injury had also brought on a bout of amnesia. Dominic's eyes widened and his pupils became enlarged as the full comprehension of his past misdeeds sank into his distraught, broken mind. Charles stopped at that point as he didn't want to overload him with any more recollections of his past misdemeanours; that would wait for another time or it might cause him to have a relapse. At that moment, he disliked his brother intensely but also loved him with intense at the same time. He leaned over and kissed his brother on his forehead before leaving. "I'll be back later and try to get some sleep in the meantime." He smiled and left the room knowing Dominic will digest every word he had spoken before hopefully chewing them over in disgust and not metaphorically spitting them out without a care.

He found Sadie and Helena waiting for him in the reception area. As he approached, Sadie quizzically asked him if *everything* had been okay, with the stress on the 'everything'. "If you mean, did I inform him that I knew of your dirty little secret? No. I'm leaving that snippet of information for later when he is a bit stronger. I've already given him much to think about. Now, let's have something to eat, for God's sake!" Helena suggested they should find a place to eat brunch as it was far too early for lunch but she was starving as she had just given all her blood away. Well half of it at least! She had added dramatically.

Their moods noticeably improved after they had eaten a decent meal and so satisfied by having full stomachs, they decided as they were in the capital of Austria, it would be remiss of them not to explore it further and become bona fide tourists and indulge in a spot of sightseeing. Charles knew things would never be the same again, but for now he had to swallow his pride and come to terms with having a dysfunctional family.

The weak November sun rays intermittently highlighted the light snow flurries that were falling gently on their hair and on their eyelashes and enhanced their spirits further. Childlike, Helena tried to catch a rogue snowflake on her tongue, as she had done when she *had* been a child.

Chapter Forty-Two

Emma laid on her back staring at the stippled white ceiling above her, reluctant to get out of bed. She had awoken early but felt she had nothing to get up for. Her life had become predictable; an anti-climax. She wanted to feel the adrenaline high that Alice was now engulfed in. Would *she* ever feel that way? Alice had returned from Bratislava the previous evening but had gone with Karl straight to his apartment. He had been worried about leaving his cat over the weekend and she had then decided to stay the night, but only if Emma didn't mind? She had added hastily. But she *had* minded. She couldn't tell Alice that, especially after she had greatly enthused about the marvellous time they had had with Karl treating her like a princess. And so, with a despondent heavy heart, she threw back the duvet and forced herself to face the day ahead. "Positive Mental Attitude!" she repeated this mantra during her shower in the hope that the hot water would wash away her negativity. She had just stepped out of the shower when she heard her mobile phone ringing. She rushed to answer it in case whoever was calling had been trying a long time and was about to ring off. It could be important, but in her haste, she had almost slipped on the wet tiled floor. Grabbing the white bath towel that had been hanging on a hook on the back of the bathroom door, to regain her balance as well as to cover her modesty, she found the culprit vibrating and still ringing for her attention on top of the bedside table. "Hello?" she answered breathlessly, as she tried to recover her composure from the assault course she had just experienced.

"Is that Emma Fogle? It is Lydia here from The Belvedere. We would like to discuss the artwork you kindly brought to our attention. Are you able to come here this afternoon, perhaps? Around three would be perfect."

"Yes, that would be ideal for me too. I will look forward to seeing you then." Emma replied in her most eloquently official voice. Immediately, after she had hung up on Lydia's call, she dialled Charles' number. *It would be good to have some support, after all, he had offered,* she thought to herself as she waited for him to answer. He had been having an early lunch with Sadie and Helena, when he had answered and stressed how pleased he was that she had asked him to accompany her to her appointment at The Belvedere. "I'll meet you there just before three, then." They agreed and suddenly, there was a purpose to the day ahead, for them both.

Charles had visited The Belvedere once before, about twenty years ago when he had not long opened 'The Hadley Gallery'. At that time, he had needed to research paintings by Egon Schiele, a contemporary of Gustav Klimt's. He was looking forward to having another reason to visit until Helena, much to his dismay, had uncharacteristically chosen to go with him. "What a good idea!" Sadie agreed, as she added that she would then be able to shop in peace without the distraction of her daughter.

"Surely, you would prefer to be with your mother rather than visit a stuffy museum." He said trying to dissuade her, but alas, it had no effect and she still insisted on being with him.

Emma was, therefore, most surprised to see Charles with Helena in tow turn up for such an important meeting. As far as Emma was concerned, it wasn't ideal to have a child present; although she knew Helena was considered an adult even if she didn't always act like one. It was difficult for Emma to disguise her annoyance and her expression must have shown this, as Charles pre-empted any awkwardness by apologising profusely and ensured Helena would behave correctly as he had already insisted that she should do so or she would have to stay in the car. Reluctantly reassured, Emma introduced them both to Lydia as they all shook hands and then followed her to the office/workroom that Emma had been shown into on her previous first visit.

Perched on an easel and directly in front of them as they entered the room was Viktor's sketch of 'The Kiss'. Charles gasped at seeing it again. He felt uneasy at remembering how it had slipped through his gallery's fingers; or to be exact, his own brother's fingers; at that thought and with renewed anger, he felt the heat of his blood rising and hoped it wouldn't show as blushing. But Lydia had begun talking and hadn't been aware of his discomfort. She was explaining to Emma that the sketch had been shown to their research and review panel for authentication who had coincidentally, been convening the very next day after Emma had brought the sketch to their attention. Charles had a feeling there was a 'but' coming and looked towards Emma anxiously. Hesitantly, Lydia proceeded to explain in further detail. "I am sorry to have to tell you but after studying and discussing the sketch thoroughly and comparing it with Klimt's catalogue raisonné, there was much deliberation but unfortunately, they found no compelling reason to believe it to be a genuine Gustav Klimt drawing."

Shocked by this unexpected revelation, Emma cried out, "It can't be right! Viktor Bloom, the owner of it, knows the exact provenance. His father had been given it as a gift from Klimt himself."

"Your friend, Viktor is probably correct but for one thing. The hand of Gustav Klimt had not sketched this. It is a good copy. More than likely the artist would have been one of his assistants or a fellow artist who had been part of the 'Secession' with Klimt at that time; a prominent new group of avant-garde artists. Please, do not be too upset by this," Lydia went on to say, "it is still a fine drawing but only worth a small fraction that a work by Klimt would have fetched. Possibly, it might achieve around 500 euros."

Helena had been absorbing everything that had been said, and without thinking of the consequences she blurted out, "I was lucky then to have got £900 for it when I sold it to the pawnbroker!" As soon as the words had flown out of her mouth, she realised she had implicated herself. Both Charles and Emma were shocked by this new piece of disclosure. Emma had had her suspicions but was always unable to prove that Helena had been completely involved in the theft. But Charles had no idea that his *daughter* had been totally complicit and had even framed Emma for the deed and to exonerate herself in the bargain. Without a doubt, she was definitely Dominic's daughter, through and through; or colloquially, the *apple didn't fall far from the tree*. Furiously, Charles dragged Helena out of the room and away from any further embarrassment. Rage got the better of him. He wanted to slap her for the hurt she had caused everyone, but knew he would be in great trouble if he did. Instead, bitter words flew out of his mouth.

"I despise your selfishness and greed and you do *not* seem to possess one iota of a conscience. I do not even want to look at you! As from now, Helena, I am wiping my hands of you and you can please yourself as to where you will live. But suffice it to say, it will not be with me! Perhaps, you should live with your true father as his blood most definitely surges through your veins." He left her standing in front of the museum bewildered by his outburst and too traumatised to cry.

Still flabbergasted with this unexpected information that Viktor's beloved sketch was a fake, Emma thanked and shook Lydia's hand anyway, as if she had been programmed too, like an automaton. She left the building clutching the sketch in a daze, making no sense of the words she had just heard that now jumbled for recognition in her brain. Helena's unexpected confession had added to that mire. "Now what shall I do! How will I tell poor Viktor?" It was all she kept thinking and loudly saying to herself. Helena had been waiting for her to appear and sheepishly informed her that Charles had 'thrown a wobbler' and had stormed off. "I don't blame him! I should do the same, but I won't. I should hate you, Helena, but deep down, I actually feel sorry for you. Unless you mend your nasty ways, you'll be devoid of friends and any family you do have. In other words, grow up and become a better person."

They sat in silence. It was only when the taxi dropped Helena at her hotel, did she apologise to Emma. "I'm truly sorry, Emma. Please forgive me!"

"It's Charles you need to apologise to, but I'm not sure he will forgive you even if I do. Goodbye, Helena."

Chapter Forty-Three

Thankfully, Alice and Karl were at the hotel when Emma arrived back. They could see immediately all was not right with her. She was ashen and speechless. And as much as they tried to encourage her to open up and include them with what seemed to be a major disaster, she just mumbled and became incoherent, with a dazed expression. Karl quickly rang room service and asked for a pot of strong coffee and a brandy to be brought to their room as soon as possible. Within ten minutes, they were insisting she should swallow the brandy with one gulp. The colour to her complexion immediately returned, mainly due to her coughing and spluttering from the shock of the potent liquid hitting her stomach. The coffee she was allowed to drink slowly as it had been too hot, and by then, she was beginning to recover her equilibrium. And the Emma they recognised had returned.

"Whatever is wrong, Emma? You must tell us as it's obviously bad news." Alice insisted with her arm round Emma's shoulders for comfort. Word for word Emma re-enacted the meeting she had had at The Belvedere, including also Helena's interesting snippet of information. "So, we were right! She did steal it from the safe and then sell it to the pawnbroker." Alice said, angrily remembering seeing it in the window of the shop.

"Yes, and unfortunately, she is the only one that has benefitted from all this; having received a remuneration far more than it was worth, apparently. Perhaps, it does pay to be dishonest!" Emma despondently shrugged her shoulders, stood up and went to look out of the window. "Viktor needs to know; he is going to be devastated. I just hope his heart will be able to take this latest traumatic news."

Emma needed some fresh air after all that coffee. By now, the sun was slowly sinking and just the last few pink rays were peeking from out of the horizon; a cool breeze was corralling the few remaining dead leaves along with a lone plastic bag and some sweet wrappers into a corner of the hotel car park. She knew Viktor would be awake now after having his usual afternoon nap and was probably enjoying a cup of tea from one of his bone China tea cups. She could visualise him now sitting with his 'friend' Hannah next to an open coal fire in his dining room and she felt guilty that she was about to disturb this peaceful scene. As the time difference would be only one hour, it was the perfect moment to call him. That's if there was a perfect moment for bad news! Hesitantly, she dialled his number and with her own heart racing, she waited for it to be answered. Hannah answered. "Viktor's in hospital again, Emma. He was rushed in yesterday with what he had insisted was indigestion but the paramedics came and said it was angina. And at his age, they were adamant that he would have to go to hospital." Hannah ensured Emma that he had had a good, comfortable night and he was being monitored.

"Please keep me informed and I'll be coming home soon. Give Viktor my best wishes, Hannah, and feed him some of your delicious chicken soup to help him recover." She said anxiously before ending the call. "I'll be glad when this day is over as that's the third piece of bad news I've heard and hopefully, it will be the last." She decided to go for a short walk to clear her mind as so much had happened in one afternoon that she needed to put it all in perspective.

She hadn't gone far when she realised a car had pulled up alongside her. Her thoughts had been elsewhere trying to fathom out her next move as if she was part of a chess game with herself playing a pawn; how appropriate and ironic. She had continued walking until she heard a man's voice asking her to stop. It was Charles. He had needed to talk to her urgently and had come by the hotel when he had seen her walking off in the opposite direction. "Please get in." He said, closing his window and reaching over to open the passenger door. She wondered what he wanted to say to her, but nevertheless she acquiesced and got into the car.

He was feeling that Emma was his only ally. The only one he was able to talk honestly to and perhaps receive some much-needed empathy from. He drove a short while not really knowing where he was headed. For some reason, subconsciously, they ended up back at The Belvedere; as if the car had been in control and had made that decision for them. It felt safe here, away from angst and arguments. It gave an impression of spatial awareness, non-claustrophobic, somewhere to de-clutter a confused mind. As they walked in the immaculate, landscaped gardens, Charles began apologising to Emma for abandoning her, as he put it, in her hour of need. He explained that his temper had been stoked out of control by Helena's lies and walking away had been the only option to diffuse

164

and dampen the situation. He continued to unburden his thoughts by saying that he cannot forgive Helena this time, as it made him wonder what other devious things she might have done without his knowledge.

Emma allowed him to express his anger and hoped it would enable him to think more rationally as to the decisions he would make about his future. They continued walking in the direction of the fountain. She noticed the effervescent display of water that had been dancing in the weak sunlight she had witnessed on her first visit to the gardens, was missing. *Perhaps, now it was getting colder and the winter had definitely arrived, it had been deactivated before becoming frozen,* she thought to herself. She agreed with him that Helena was a force to be reckoned with, a definite problem child and that she had tried telling her that she needed to improve her ways. But would his conscience allow him to completely wash his hands of her?

"I have given her everything. I raised her as my own and she had the best education I could afford. She had wanted for nothing but now it is Dominic's turn to be a good father to her, if that would be at all possible. My mind is made up, Emma. I'm going to divorce Sadie as I can't trust her either! She hadn't been honest with me from the very beginning. Apparently, she had wanted Dominic to marry her, once she knew she was carrying his child, but he had refused and had even questioned whether the baby was his."

"Are you sure that's what you want? Have you told her?"

"Not yet, but I will when we get back. I have decided not to procrastinate, it needs urgent action for my life to improve; like a surgical operation to remove dead tissue and improve one's health."

Shocked at Charles' vehemence, Emma informed him that she will be returning to London as soon as possible. She needed to visit Viktor as he was once again in hospital and to return his artwork to him. Although he might not want it back when he learns it is not a genuine Klimt.

"I will be willing to buy it from him if he wishes to sell it and give him a decent price for it as compensation for all the aggravation he has had to endure, poor man."

"That's very kind of you but I'm not sure he would want to sell it as his father had given it to him and although it might not be worth as much now in monetary terms, the sentimental value is more important to him and always was." Emma sighed, thinking of how proud Viktor had been when he had shown the sketch to her and Dominic. And now, she was dreading deflating him with this latest revelation.

Their feet had intuitively brought them to the entrance of the building, without them both realising the urge they had to see the original painting of 'The Kiss' again. Lydia had seen them walk past her office window and had come out to greet them and asked if they were wishing to see her again. They apologised for unintentionally disturbing her but wondered if they could view Klimt's paintings once more before leaving for London? Escorting them up to the floor the gallery was situated on, she left them in private, but not before telling them they could take their time. They were alone in this huge room and felt privileged not having to share this experience with any strangers. Standing with Charles and looking up at this magnificently painted work of art, Emma's eyes captured the intensity of the bond between the lovers. It never failed to leave her emotionally lightheaded. Charles could see she was captivated and agreed it was a magnificent example of the 'Art Nouveau' period. It seemed to inspire him to become assertive and forthright.

"Come back with me to London, Emma, and please take up my offer to work in 'The Hadley' with me again. Helena will no longer be working there and Dominic will be out of action for a long while. You can be my personal assistant; we can run it together."

"I'm not sure, Charles. I'll have to think about it."

"What if the company sends you with all expenses paid, to study here in Vienna at The Belvedere for three weeks or a month if necessary? For you to study all of Klimt's paintings but especially this one! You can then specialise in this period of Austrian art which Klimt became famous for and be an asset to my gallery. I will arrange it with Lydia, if you say yes."

Emma could see the excitement in Charles' eyes at the possible prospect of this union between them. He had become so animated with enthusiasm she felt she was unable to refuse such a fantastic offer. "Yes, Charles," she finally said after a deliberated pause. "I will accept your wonderful offer as this means I will always be a part of the magic that Vienna offers, with Gustav Klimt as its soul."

Chapter Forty-Four

She had rushed to tell Alice her news as soon as Charles had dropped her off at the hotel. Karl hadn't been there. He had decided he should start working again as he had a wedding to pay for in the near future and his savings were at an all-time low. Alice was thrilled that Emma had finally accepted Charles' offer and what a fantastic offer it was and a definite step up the proverbial ladder. Alice's eyes suddenly clouded over and a pained expression distorted her usually bright, gamine features. "I will miss you so much, Emma. It will be hard to imagine not having you meet me for lunch on the spur of the moment, as we have done so many times."

"Don't be too sad, with this new job, it seems I'll be here more often than you think. We might even be seeing each other more than ever and then you'll be fed up with me!" Laughing to cheer her friend up, Emma gave her a hug and enthused on all Alice had to look forward to. "I hope I'll still be your matron of honour at your wedding? And hopefully, by then I'll have a plus one to escort me there." She added, showing Alice her crossed fingers on both her hands for extra luck.

"When are you leaving to return to London?"

"Charles wishes to travel back with me, so as soon as he drops the bombshell to Sadie that he is divorcing her, he will arrange the plane tickets. Perhaps, I had better start packing now as he might want to escape the inevitable fallout!"

Emma was right. Now he had decided on a definite plan of action, Charles didn't want to wait a moment longer than necessary. He told Sadie about his wishes for a divorce and methodically informed her as to how it would be, for both of them. He would willingly give her the house and most of its contents as he would be buying an apartment nearer to his gallery in Covent Garden.

"You've got it all worked out nicely, haven't you?" Sadie bitterly replied, trying not to breakdown. "What if *I* do not want a divorce?"

"That is up to you. But I will be visiting my solicitor as soon as I get back and it will be in your interests to agree or he might suggest I will be foolish to give you the house and not fight for half the assets."

"And what do you propose to do about Dominic?" Sadie sneered. "You can't just abandon him!"

"I do *not* intend to and unless you want to look after him, after all he was once your lover, I will be transferring him to have private care in London. Is that agreeable with you?"

Sadie finally broke down and was unable to answer. He had become so aloof. Her misery had no effect on him. Her once kind, compassionate husband had now been replaced by an imposter. Where once her crying would have softened him, it now had the opposite effect and he just stood stiff and upright like an oak, unyielding against external elements.

She had always loved Dominic more than Charles; he had seduced her with his handsome, almost model looks and his cheekiness. She knew he was a chancer and not the type to rely on but she couldn't help herself. He had been forbidden fruit and that always tasted better for having scrumped it, but once consumed she should have seen the maggot inside. Her scheming, once she found out that she was pregnant, worked and she had netted Charles. It had taken roughly four years but the hard work of rising to his standards with the help of tedious beauty regimes, cookery lessons and not to forget fake orgasms, finally convinced him to propose to her. Good, solid Charles, the complete opposite of his brother. But the chemistry had never been there. She had been a good actress; hence the fake orgasms and he had never been made aware of her true love. She had managed to deceive him for almost fifteen years playing the perfect wife; for the sake of her daughter, she had maintained that pretence. But she knew that one day, the truth would be out. She had hoped it would last a bit longer, at least until Helena had left home or had become married. Then, she could have chosen her time for a divorce, at *her* behest. Perhaps, Dominic would have entered this fantasy and realised his latent love for her and resumed their once amorous liaison. Not that she would want that now! Not in his present state of health. So perhaps, after all, she had made the right choice.

Charles left Sadie contemplating her next move. But generously, he felt, he had offered to include both her and Helena in purchasing return tickets to London for them also. That was whether they had wanted to leave at the same time as him or not. It hadn't mattered, but he knew he couldn't leave them stranded, he wasn't that heartless. All that was left for him to organise now was Dominic. Driving to the hospital, Charles pondered over the last few days that seemed to have stretched to a year in his mind due to the traumatic content that had filled those hours. He realised now that he hardly knew his own brother. In all good faith, he had taken him on as a partner in the gallery convinced that he had been honest and reliable; the perfect combination to go into business with. And together with his affability and confidence, it seemed a sure thing. Instead, his true self has been revealed. Not only had he been proved to be a liar but also a devious thief. "And I fell for all his lies!" He said, loudly to no one but himself, to justify this statement. "But he is still my brother and I *am* the eldest, I have to do the right thing and help him, regardless." It reminded Charles of a passage in the Bible between two brothers. Was it Jacob and Esau? He wasn't sure, but there were always conflicts and then forgiveness. He wasn't ready just yet to forgive Dominic but hopefully one day, if he mended his ways, it might happen. But that would be further down the line and for now the important thing was to get him back to London and for him to make a full recovery.

Opening the door to Dominic's hospital room, he was surprised to see his brother sitting out of the bed and in the vinyl-covered armchair next to it and with a blanket round his shoulders for warmth as the small window above the bed had been left open. All the intrusive tubes had been removed and he looked more like his old self apart from the slight slackness on the right-side of his face. Dominic gave a crooked smile when Charles came over to greet him. He tried to speak but his words were still slurred. Tears began forming in his eyes, which over-spilled down his cheeks and then dripped haphazardly onto his legs, causing small saline spots to fleetingly stain his pyjamas. He automatically tried to wipe them away but his right arm wouldn't allow him to. Charles could see the anguish his brother was feeling and at that moment he knew he wanted to help him, he had to, there was no-one else for the job.

The door suddenly burst open with such force that it knocked a trolley over, containing surgical masks and other required medical ephemera, as it caught its back wheel and sent it spinning. The cacophony of the metal trays hitting the tiled flooring seemed louder than any orchestra rehearsing Pomp and Circumstance that Charles had ever heard. They both jumped at the noise, Dominic painfully. A very angry Sadie had entered the room in the most dramatic way. She hadn't been sure if Charles would be there, but she was past caring now, all had been revealed. She needed to confront Dominic and have her say, to his face.

"I despise you for ruining my marriage and devastating my life! To think I actually loved you and had wanted us to marry when I knew I was pregnant with Helena. You are and always will be a selfish bastard. Never once did you allow yourself to show affection for her other than when it suited, of late, to induct her into your nefarious schemes. But still…," and here she paused to get her breath, "you have now received your comeuppance and are being punished for your past bad behaviour." The outpouring of home truths that had been building up inside her had finally reached their crescendo. She stopped exhausted and realised then she had had an audience. The doctor as well as two nurses had come running after they had heard the dreadful disturbance emanating from Dominic's room. Sadie felt drained of all emotion. She felt weak and her legs began to wobble, she knew she was about to faint. Fortunately, the doctor had pre-empted this from happening by catching her and holding her steady whilst a nurse placed a chair under her to sit on. Her head was placed between her knees, in a most undignified manner, but was necessary for the blood to rush back to her brain.

Apologising for his wife's outburst, Charles spoke to the doctor about arranging for Dominic to be discharged the following day. He fully explained his plan to him to have his brother cared for privately in London. Therefore, he would be grateful if they could have all his medical notes ready by tomorrow when he came to collect him. Once the doctor had agreed to this sudden rearrangement, Charles shook his hand and walked away, leaving Sadie still recovering from her verbal explosion. He had understood the anger she had directed at Dominic, but knew deep down, she had been angrier at herself.

Chapter Forty-Five

Emma arrived at the airport earlier than she had intended. Saying goodbye to Alice had had them both in tears and she hadn't wanted to drag it out any further. She had waited for Karl to arrive before leaving so that her dear friend wouldn't be left on her own. Emma was pleased to know that Alice was moving in with Karl that day, which had made sense. She knew it would be a testing time for them both, but as they were so deeply in love with each other, it couldn't possibly go wrong. Relieved at how things were finally working out for other people, she now had to devote her time and energies to her own future; which seemed to be heading in the right direction, after all, being a PA in The Hadley Gallery was definitely going to be a step up. *And* she won't have Helena there to make her feel intimidated. That had sealed the deal! But despite the promise of a rosy future ahead of her, she still had a gnawing feeling inside her as if she was constantly hungry and no matter what she ate wouldn't satisfy that hunger, the emptiness. It then dawned on her that it was the magic of Vienna and its exquisite art, mainly Klimt, that she craved and loved; the mere thought of 'The Kiss' made her mouth water and left her wanting more, insatiable, as if she was a mistress weak with desire. For a moment, she had forgotten where she was, and then reality kicked in; this wouldn't be goodbye, but adieu for now, as she would soon be returning to study all of Klimt's masterpieces.

With a wide smile on her face, as she was considering these positive thoughts and images, she looked up to see Charles pushing a wheelchair, containing a slumped Dominic, across the airport concourse. She waved to attract his attention. She saw him smile back and return her wave. And there was no sign of Sadie or Helena much to her relief, only a porter assisting them with their suitcases. It was disconcerting seeing Dominic so helpless; he seemed to have shrunk, probably because he was unable to sit upright and his once fine, tanned complexion was now sallow which had enhanced the lines on his face and exaggerated his age. He now looked like the older brother.

He wouldn't meet her eyes. He didn't want to see pity in them. He still had a modicum of self-respect left even though he knew he would now be treated as an invalid, which of course was exactly what he was. Sadie had been spot-on in her retribution speech the day before. The word 'comeuppance' had weighed heavily on his mind all night. Perhaps, there is such a thing and it was now his turn to suffer life's indignities. After all, hadn't he caused sufferance to others? Punishment was an even harsher word to swallow. He had never been a religious man but was a higher entity punishing him now for all his wrongdoings? And was it the time now to make amends? He knew it was and the cheating and deceiving had to end; after all, that was the reason he was now beholden to being wheeled like a baby in a pushchair. But he could use this as his rebirth, a new start! Once his health improved, and he would be determined that it shall, he would become a better person; kinder, selfless and caring for others feelings. It seemed a tall order to declare but he felt he would have the determination to see it through and now, this minute was the best way to prove it. Raising his head, he looked directly at Emma and mouthed "sorry."

Emma wasn't sure if she had heard him correctly, as a family with a young child was sitting a few seats away, and at that moment, the little girl had caught her fingers in her doll's pushchair as she had tried to collapse it and was now screaming in pain. Emma had been aware that he had lifted his head to look at her and was now trying to speak. "What did you say, Dominic? I'm sorry I couldn't hear you." He repeated his apology as he could see she had seemed confused. This time, she understood and squeezed his hand gently in reply.

They were first to board the plane as Dominic had to be assisted into his seat and his wheelchair stowed in the aircraft's hold. Charles had been assured that it will be retrieved and given back as soon as they had landed at Heathrow. He didn't relish the idea of having to carry Dominic to the cases carousel, after all, contrary to the lyrics of the song by The Hollies, he *would* be heavy. Charles explained that Sadie and Helena were returning the following day as she had not wished to travel 'en famille' as she had put it. After all, the pretence was over.

Out of the aircraft's dull, grainy windows, they could see below them dark grey, angry rainclouds heralding; they were now approaching England's airspace. They were warned by the captain, over the tannoy system, that there will be much turbulence and to keep their seatbelts securely fastened. True to his words, the aircraft seemed to be tossed around like a ship on stormy seas but in this instance, stormy skies. Nevertheless, it was still rather daunting and Emma grabbed hold of Charles' hand for reassurance just as the plane seemed to take a nose dive. They had dropped several thousand feet before it began to level out and they could at last see the patchwork of fields with soggy wet animals sheltering under dripping rain-soaked trees. The rain was now lashing hard against the glass and they silently prayed the plane wouldn't skid as it landed along the runway. With white knuckles tightly holding armrests, the entire plane of passengers seemed to hold their breath…Then, the audible sound of exhalation in unison was enough confirmation of a safe landing as the plane glided to a bumpy halt.

Once through passport control, Emma said her farewells as she was going to get the underground train home. It was a Friday afternoon and she knew she would end up being caught in the rush hour of workers leaving offices eager to begin their own weekends. Charles had informed her that he would be temporarily staying in Dominic's flat until he had found his own apartment as well as until Dominic's health had shown some improvement. He implied also that he would be expecting to see her at the gallery on Monday morning at 9.30 am as they had a lot to catch up on. And with a wink of his eye and a warm smile, he pushed Dominic towards the taxi rank.

She suddenly felt lonely, even though the carriage was jam packed. She was surrounded by other travellers jostling for space with their suitcases or pushchairs monopolising any empty floor area that happened to become available. With bruised shins and sore toes from being trampled on, Emma was delighted when the next stop that had just been announced, was hers. Now all she had to do would be to fight her way through the throng before the doors closed. Apologising for knocking into reluctant, static, unmoveable passengers, she managed to alight onto the platform just in time. It had been like an assault course for her. With this ungainly, tortured experience fresh in her mind and with grazed legs, she headed for the taxi rank. As she looked out of the window, the familiar suburbs of London flashed by; each with their own rows of regimented, semi-detached or terraced houses, with double-glazed windows and the obligatory concreted front gardens. Neat but boring, she observed. Whether it is Ruislip or Edgware, they all looked similar and must be confusing to an out-of-town visitor. It had been a wrench for her to temporarily leave Vienna with its stunning pristine white architecture.

Her mum had been waiting by the window, nervously watching any movement outside that could herald the return of her daughter. As soon as she heard and then saw the taxi pull up, she rushed to open the front door. It had been a long, worrying time since Emma had left for Vienna and now, she was thankful she was safely back with her. But knowing her daughter's adventurous spirit, she expected it wouldn't be for long. Her mum's embrace was most welcoming after such an exhausting, challenging day, both mentally and physically. They sat together for the remainder of the day, drinking copious amounts of tea and devouring delicious home-made food, whilst Emma related, in as much detail as she could remember, all that had occurred in the last few weeks. Surprised to learn of Alice's impending marriage, her mum wondered if Emma, herself, had found romance. "I did," she sighed, but it was with the city and an enchanting painting called "'The Kiss'." Disappointed, her mother replied, "So, I guess I don't need to buy a new outfit just yet?"

"No, not yet! Not for a long while." She apologised.

Chapter Forty-Six

Apart from using the entire weekend to recover before beginning work on the following Monday, Emma needed to speak to Hannah to find out whether Viktor was still in hospital. She prayed silently that his health had improved so that he would now be at home. After enjoying a much-needed nine hours sleep, she had a lazy breakfast of buttered toast oozing with honey and a mug of strong percolated coffee, showered, and then gave Hannah the call she had been dreading in case she heard bad news. "Hello, Hannah, it's me Emma. How is Viktor?" Emma was relieved to hear that Viktor was now out of hospital and had been discharged the day before on condition he wouldn't over exert himself.

But as Hannah stressed sarcastically, "He never exerts himself! I exert it for him!" Emma could hear the fondness in her tone despite her trying to cover it up with indignant mockery.

"Would he be up to me visiting him tomorrow?" Emma asked warily. Hannah agreed on the proviso it would be a short visit as he needed much rest and no excitement. Promising she would make sure the latter wouldn't occur, Emma said she would look forward to seeing them both the following day.

It seemed a life time ago that she was last ringing their doorbell. So much had happened in the pursuit of Viktor's lost sketch. Had it been worth it? Probably not, as it had proved to be a fake and poor, dear Alice had suffered abduction and physical abuse at the hands of a ruthless criminal, for its return. These thoughts were whirling in her mind whilst she was waiting for Hannah to eventually open the door. She knew she had to be economical with the truth and to select only certain details of how the sketch had finally been recovered. "I mustn't upset him with all the facts." She muttered as Hannah at last opened the door and welcomed her inside.

"I'm sorry making you wait but I was washing vegetables in the kitchen sink with the tap running. You must have knocked a few times before I had realised someone was outside. Please forgive me!" Reassuring Hannah that she was forgiven, Emma followed her into the familiar dining room where Viktor now spent most of his day. He must have been asleep or perhaps dozing; as he sensed he had a visitor, he opened his eyes abruptly just as Emma gingerly tiptoed towards him, fearful of waking him.

"Hello, Viktor." She whispered in case he had wanted to resume his nap. Instead, he held out his hands and beckoned her to move closer to him. She could see immediately the toll the last heart incident had played on his health. His once bright blue eyes had now become dull grey and rheumy. He reached out to pluck a fresh tissue from a box sitting on a side table next to him. "These are my constant companions." He said jokingly as he wiped the lacrimal overspill that had begun to flow from the corner of each eye. "If it's not my eyes that need wiping, then it's my nose; I believe they're in constant competition with each other. Either way it's a nuisance!" Emma was pleased that Viktor had retained his sense of humour and waited for him to complete his ritual before proceeding to the matter of his sketch.

She handed the perfectly wrapped parcel to him without saying a word. There were no words, she felt that could explain the huge disappointment that she had endured at being informed that it was a fake. She knew if she was upset then Viktor must be devastated and maybe, that had caused his latest angina attack. Nevertheless, he started carefully to unwrap it with adroit, bony fingers, until at last, his beloved sketch was revealed to him as he had remembered it. Thankful to have it returned and in perfect condition, he kissed it gently; as if it was a former lover that had been parted from him for an enforced long time due to a war and had now been reunited. After witnessing this surprising show of emotion, Emma was even more surprised when Viktor handed the sketch back to her.

"I want you to have it, Emma." He said thoughtfully. "Not because I know now that it isn't worth as much as I had expected, but because it still means so much to me and I have no one I would rather leave it with than you. I would like you to treasure it as I have done; obviously not for the same reasons, but because of its history. Whether Klimt himself had drawn it or not, it had been given to my father by another artist from the same studio, one of his assistants, a protégé of his." A fit of coughing brought Viktor's soliloquy to an abrupt end and Emma quickly called out to Hannah for assistance. Thankfully, the coughing fit had subsided as soon as Hannah brought in a tray of tea and freshly-made kichals (biscuits) along with Viktor's asthma pump. She handed him the pump which he reluctantly took from her. "This makes me feel like I'm an old man!" He said objecting to her helping him place it over his airwaves. "You *are* an old man!" She quipped.

Their good humour continued throughout the rest of the afternoon even after Emma had recounted the ordeals they had had to overcome. He was pleased that her friend, Alice, had found the love of her life and was marrying a Viennese; the handsomest men in the world, he stated with a cheeky smile. Even though he had never met Charles, he was upset to learn that his marriage had come to a dramatic end. But he gave a beaming smile, which for a moment recaptured a glimpse of his Azure blue eyes that made him look younger, when he learnt of Emma's new position in the gallery.

"You must be thrilled!" They both exclaimed to Emma. "At least, something good came out of all of this." She agreed with them and explained that it would involve her visiting Vienna often as Charles would like her to become extremely knowledgeable regarding Viennese artists, especially Klimt. In fact, she would be returning quite soon to study at The Belvedere. And she confessed to them that her heart was still there. A far-away look crossed Viktor's face, "That city captures you. Even though, I had left there when I was a very young child, I had visited often in the past, to see my family. I would go back in a heartbeat. But my heart's not beating as good nowadays, and so, I daren't try." He said with a heavy sigh and wiped first his eyes and then his nose with another clean tissue he had extracted from the little, green tissue box.

Emma could see he was beginning to flag and was trying hard not to close his eyes. Ever ready to protect him, Hannah jumped up and busied herself gathering the dirty cups onto the tray; Emma took this as a sign of dismissal. She thanked him again for the wonderful gift and stressed that if he should change his mind, she would gladly, but reluctantly, hand it back. His last words before she had left the room were, "It's yours, my dear, enjoy!"

Chapter Forty-Seven

Travelling the familiar route to 'The Hadley' reminded Emma of the first day she had begun working there; including the butterflies that were now swirling relentlessly inside her. Why *was* she so nervous? *That* Emma had been naïve and easily led. *Today's* Emma was assured and confident, with a sound future ahead of her; not on a three-month trial as before, but personal assistant to the boss who had had to persuade her to take the position. Nevertheless, she knew she still had to prove to him and to herself, that he had been right to offer her the job.

Stepping inside the gallery, she half expected to see Dominic's presence as he had usually been the first to arrive each morning. But of course, this was now the beginning of December; much had happened to alter the balance of sibling directorship with only Charles now at the helm. Hence, her promotion! It had only just opened and there wasn't anyone, clients or staff, to be seen. The bell over the main door had rung as she had entered, heralding a visitor. Counting silently in her head, she knew by the time she had reached five, Charles would have appeared; she wasn't disappointed.

"Emma, how wonderful!" and gave her a hug. "It's so good to have you back!" He greeted her with such enthusiasm that she blushed surprised at the informality he had always been prone to avoid. Obviously, a huge change in his own circumstances had made him more approachable and less staid. Things were definitely getting better! Even more so when he informed her that she was now to have Dominic's office as her own; which he had felt was only right, as she was after all, his PA. She spent most of that first morning removing Dominic's ephemera, but keeping back anything that she thought might be relevant for her. She found the boxes containing the books and catalogues that she had last been working on, before being rudely dismissed, in the basement where Helena had flung them haphazardly into a cupboard with an old vacuum cleaner as an unlikely companion; so obviously gloating, and eager to erase every iota of her nemesis' presence. She smiled imagining Helena's triumphant grin, but now she had had the last laugh. As she passed by her old office, an image of her and Dominic flashed through her mind. How stupid she was to think that he had fancied her. Never again will she be taken in by a handsome man! Forcing all these past imagery and negative thoughts aside, Emma carried her newly acquired belongings upstairs to her new office.

She had decided that Viktor's sketch (her sketch) would be perfect adorning one of her office walls; then she would be able to see it almost every day. It would be in appropriate surroundings, amongst other works of art and would inspire her each time she gazed upon it. Holding it up against each smooth, pale grey wall in turn, she preferred the one opposite her desk as it was furthest away from the window and therefore having no reflective light to distort or deface it. She removed a print of a racehorse by Munnings that Dominic had hung there (obviously it had inspired him to gamble) and now replaced it with her sketch. As she was standing back to admire her handiwork, Charles came in to see if she had settled in okay. He gave a low, long whistle of approval when he saw her admiring her new acquisition.

"I take it the old man has given it to you? That's marvellous!" He genuinely exclaimed, then added, "I'm still in the market to buy it from you, if you so wish?"

"Sorry, Charles, but Viktor has entrusted me with his heirloom and I promised him I would take great care of it. Anyway, I absolutely adore it. But if it's okay with you I would like to keep it here, where, despite recent history, it'll be safe and you are also aware of its meaning and provenance; its true value." Charles fully agreed and for the rest of the day, they discussed forthcoming exhibitions and events that the gallery could be included in with a catalogue of their prime pieces to be distributed to a range of reputable companies in and around London. During a break for lunch, Emma asked him how Dominic was and whether he had improved at all.

"Don't worry, he won't be back at work for a long time, if ever, I'm afraid. In fact, I have booked a private nurse to look after him each day I'm not there; hopefully, she'll be young and pretty to show him what he is missing and encourage him to improve. Horrible, aren't I?" He said mischievously with a glint in his eye. "Yes, you are!" She agreed and smiled anyway at his current light heartedness.

"Now, Emma, for the rest of this week, I would like you to help me interview possible candidates for your former position. I have already placed an advert in

'Art News', I had done this before going to Vienna and have received several replies, as I had anticipated you agreeing to my offer of promotion. Here is the list." Charles passed her the list of names for her to scrutinise along with comments of their suitability. "After all, you'll be away soon for three weeks and I will be requiring assistance to help me run this place." He said firmly back in his efficient mode.

In between interviews, Emma kept busy organising her itinerary for her three-week study course at The Belvedere, as was promised. *How incredible life can be*, she thought. It's about turn! I'm *now* interviewing the nervous candidates and questioning the statements *they* had written on *their* CVs. She could, therefore, sympathise with each one and tried to be fair and encourage their confidence. The interviews had gone well and, in the end, the final decision was Charles'. He chose a smart young lad, eager to learn the trade and was especially interested in art, even though he hadn't been to an art college; Charles didn't think that would be a disadvantage. He felt, he had said, that he would be able to mould him into a reliable, polite salesman and would be an asset to The Hadley Gallery. Where had she heard those words before?

Chapter Forty-Eight

Time was running out for Emma to get everything she needed doing before her flight in just two days. It all seemed to be happening so fast. Charles had given her the plane tickets and all she had to do was print off her boarding passes. Between Viktor and his cousin, Frederik, they had found Emma a reasonable place for her to stay during her three weeks in Vienna. It was in a reputable boarding house belonging to a friend of Frederik's wife and not too far away from where they lived. Emma knew this meant that they would be able to keep an eye on her, just in case she needed help in any way. She appreciated the care and time that all the Bloom family had taken; they had become like extended relatives with Viktor at the head, fussing over her as if she was his grandchild. Despite making her feel ten years old again, it had felt good. Their kindness was overwhelming and she was looking forward to being amongst them once more. She could feel the excitement bubbling inside her, like a whirlpool of emotion, eddying to the surface only to subside and then rise again in an instant. Not long now and I shall also be with Alice, she smiled at the thought.

Charles had handed her a printed document, methodically listing all of Klimt's works that he wanted her to study and concentrate on. "It's easy to get side-tracked when you are among such a plethora of wondrous artists." He had stated firmly. "I need you to become a fountain of knowledge for the gallery, so that we will be aware of future auction purchases from that region."

"I'm sure it will take more than three weeks for me to become anywhere near a connoisseur, Charles." She had replied amused at his faith in her ability. "Perhaps, I should stay longer then?"

"I should think not!" He reiterated, "I have already agreed to you staying for New Year's Eve and flying back the following day. Besides, I will miss you and I need you here." He added in a softer tone.

Leaving work that evening with a file of important details and contact information she will need, Emma was ecstatic to think that in less than 24 hours, she would be back where her heart was still beating. That evening, her mum had made Emma's favourite roast dinner; chicken breast with three kinds of vegetables, as well as her mouth-watering crispy roast potatoes of which she always had seconds and Yorkshire pudding with home-made gravy. It was all ready for her as she walked in. "It smells and looks delicious! I was hoping the aroma was from here and not next door as I walked up the path." Her stomach rumbled in expectation of the feast ahead.

"It's to make sure you have one decent meal to set you on your way tomorrow." Her mum answered in reply to Emma's quizzical look.

"Wine as well? I should go away more often!" She laughed as a glass of Prosecco was placed next to her plate. "Here's to a safe, happy and productive three weeks." They chinked their wine glasses together and each took a sip.

"Also, for a 'Happy New Year', as I won't be with you when it arrives." Her mum added.

"*And* not forgetting, it's a 'Happy New Millennium' also, Mum. The year 2000! Incredible!" They prematurely toasted all the forthcoming festivities Emma would be absent for, before devouring the appetising meal set in front of them.

Emma woke up the following morning with the cold, low winter sun streaming through her cotton Laura Ashley floral printed curtains. At this time of the year, the night's darkness seemed reticent to leave to make way for the dawn; it seemed to drag its heels like a child not wanting to go to school. Taking all this into account, Emma gauged that it must be around 8 am, without first looking at the clock sitting on her bedside table. The day ahead looked promising. She drew back the curtains to see a sharp frost had arrived during the latter part of the night; coating the rose bush leaves with a fine, dusting of what looked like iridescent icing sugar. In between the branches, spiders' webs had become accentuated with each fine thread a diamond necklace fit for a fairy. An enchanting scene and definitely one she would have loved to sketch any other time, but not today. Today, she had forged plans for her visit to another magical place and pretty soon, in the next few hours, she would be there.

It had been a wrench saying goodbye to her mother again after only being back just over a week. But she had known it would be a flying visit as her daughter's life had altered dramatically. She had shown how proud she was of Emma's promotion by putting £1000 into her bank account that she had been saving towards her only daughter's imaginary future wedding. Sitting on the plane, Emma recalled her mum's words, "I want you to have this now (handing her the bank receipt). Whether you keep it for security, giving you peace of mind in case an emergency should arise or you wish to spend it; either way, it's yours to enjoy and to keep you safe." She had thanked and hugged her with tears rolling down her cheeks. She knew she would wear that love and generosity as if it was a cashmere shawl that will keep her warm throughout her absence.

To see Alice waving frantically at the barrier, as she entered the concourse through the 'Nothing to Declare' double doorway, dismissed instantly any melancholy thoughts of home. Abandoning her suitcase haphazardly, so that the people behind her had to swerve to avoid falling over it, Emma rushed over to enthusiastically hug her friend. "I can't believe I'm back again!" She gushed.

"Collect your suitcase before the authorities decide it's suspicious and remove it for you!" Alice shouted above the cacophony of other excited travellers reuniting with their own loved ones.

"Where's Karl?" Emma asked dragging her re-acclaimed suitcase behind her.

"He's sitting outside in the car as he refused to pay the extortionate price for parking. Come on, he's at the drop off point." Emma duly followed Alice to the car. Karl greeted Emma with a kiss on both cheeks, opened the door for her and then opened the boot of the car for her case. "Let's get home before it snows." He said pointing at the heavy, grey sky. "It has been getting colder each day and the forecast is for much snow this month." He sounded so much like an official meteorological reporter that they both laughed at him without him knowing why. Emma went back to Karl's, (their), apartment for lunch and to catch up on all their news. "Well? You must have something new to tell me." She asked, as Karl's cat had made itself comfortable on her lap while pushing its head against her hand to initiate being stroked.

"We have, but we weren't going to tell you immediately." Emma looked intrigued at Alice's hint of something momentous about to be revealed. "We've decided to get married as soon as possible; this month, preferably New Year's Eve."

"That would be ideal for me! I can help you with any arrangements *and* I will definitely be here to be your maid of honour. Perfect! We'll have to start shopping for dresses." Excited by this revelation, Emma for that moment had forgotten the real reason she had been sent there; which was to work. "Have you booked the venue, yet?" she asked.

"Not yet. Karl dropped the bombshell on me only last night and I'm still getting used to the idea. He thought it would be romantic to get married at the very beginning of a new millennium; to symbolise our enduring love. Now, the problem is, we have to find a venue at such short notice!" Alice stressed, waiting for Karl to respond. Karl explained that he would be contacting the Vienna City Hall to enquire whether they have availability on that day; or whether it will even be open for ceremonies, but being a weekday, a Friday, it might well be. He had sounded hopeful.

"That sounds wonderful, fingers crossed you'll be able to book it. You never know they might have a cancellation. But now, would you be able to take me to my boarding house? I need to settle in and get organised for tomorrow. Charles has instructed me on maintaining an efficient work schedule and I can't let him down." She said with a wry smile and raised eyebrows.

They helped Emma into her bedsit after the initial warm welcome from the landlady; who had insisted on a genial cup of tea, or maybe something stronger if you prefer? Emma chose the former as she didn't want to give the wrong impression on her first day there and anyway, perhaps it had been a test to see which one she *would* choose. It was a compact but a basic, spotlessly clean room with all the essentials for her stay there to be a reasonably comfortable one. At least, it was bright with a south facing window that looked over the fairly large garden at the back of the building. The snow, that Karl had forecasted, was now beginning to swirl down heavily outside. Large snowflakes were beating against the glass, and then sliding down to form a crystallised layer on top of the window ledge; which, she knew, would harden into packed ice and force the window to remain shut until the thaw. A small radiator next to the bed made the room feel snug and cosy. Satisfied with her new surroundings, Emma thanked her friends, but now she wanted to unpack and then hopefully go for a walk to get her bearings for tomorrow's journey to The Belvedere; that's if she won't be snowed in.

The landlady, Mrs Katz, had opened the door to the communal bathroom as they had ascended the stairs when first being shown the layout of the house. That had been the only downside for Emma; having to share a loo and a shower. Still, being winter, there was only one other guest in residence, she had been informed, so there shouldn't ever be a queue for the use of the facilities. With this thought in her mind, she half wondered who the other guest was and would they meet? But what she needed now was a map of the area and directions on getting to work the next day. She could hear Mrs Katz talking downstairs and hoped she wouldn't mind her bothering her. Knocking on the door, she waited. The silence lasted ten seconds before the door flung open and a tall, blond and extremely handsome, young man stood framed in the doorway as if he had just stepped into a masterpiece. Well, she hadn't expected that!

Chapter Forty-Nine

"Guten Tag." (Good day) He announced with a wide smile showing perfect white teeth below the beginnings of a fair and slightly gingery moustache. "Hello." Emma replied hesitantly, surprised that he was not Mrs Katz. Blushing she explained her reason for disturbing them. "Please excuse my manners. Do come in!" He said in precise English with a strong Austrian accent and gestured with his arms for her to enter. Mrs Katz was sitting by a coal fire with a newspaper strewn by her feet that had obviously fallen off her lap when she had dozed off. Emma entering the room had awoken her with a start and she hurried to gather it up.

"I see you have met my son, Gustav." She said in a sleepy voice whilst trying to clear her throat. "He is the only other person staying here at this moment." She added as further explanation. This time, he held out a hand for her to shake to confirm his mother's informal introduction. His hand felt cool as he gripped hers firmly; his long, tapered fingers surrounded her hand in a powerful gesture.

"Please to meet you." Emma garbled, slightly stunned and lost for words and momentarily forgetting the reason she had knocked. "I…I wonder if you have a map of the city I could borrow until I buy one tomorrow." She remembered suddenly.

He walked over to a bookcase and opened one of two drawers at the bottom of it and handed her a map. "You are welcome to keep it as we have a few of them we give out to our guests, should they request one." She thanked him and apologised for disturbing their peace and turned to go. He quickly added, "My mother informed me you are here to study at The Belvedere for a short time. I, myself have a degree in art history and I would be happy to take you in my car tomorrow, for your first day. I can then, if you so wish, point out the tram route you would need to take each day." She decided to take him up on his offer. Why not? He might prove useful; a kindred spirit and with a degree in art, perhaps he could help my career and him being an Adonis would definitely be an added bonus. She mused on these wicked thoughts, before thanking him and arranging a time for the morning.

It had snowed heavily throughout the night and Emma was concerned that she wouldn't be able to get to the museum. Looking out of the window, the snow looked to be at least 30 centimetres deep with drifts as high as the garden wall. The trees appeared like silhouettes against the stark, eerily quiet background with a uniform thick white stripe down one side of each trunk, like soldiers on parade. She could hear much shovelling in progress out in the street. Collecting her tote bag, she went downstairs to find Gustav had already cleared a pathway to his car. Sweating profusely from the exertion, he explained that no one in Vienna would be seen all winter if they let a little bit of snow force them to remain indoors, and all the cars had snow tyres, as it was the law. Relieved, Emma jumped into the passenger seat at his request.

She made notes of all the tram numbers and stops she would be using during her stay; and imagined herself travelling on one of these antennaed, caterpillar-like machines and looking out of a steamed-up window. Gustav behaved like a tour guide, eager to give a brief insight to the history of Klimt; his rise as a renowned artist and his association with his long-time model and rumoured lover, Emilie Flöge. Looking at Emma's profile, as he was driving, he suddenly exclaimed, "That is it! That is why you looked familiar to me. You share a likeness to *her*, Emilie! I have studied many photographs and writings about them, so I consider myself an expert." He excitedly said, pleased at his own deduction.

"I've been told that before by a very old gentleman whose father had worked in Klimt's studio." She then regaled the story of the sketch and the photo that Viktor had given her. By this time, they had arrived at the gates of The Belvedere. Thanking him she said she would see him back at the house later that afternoon and walked into the entrance hall to be greeted by Lydia as if she was an old friend.

"How pleased we are that you will be spending three weeks with us." She said guiding Emma into her office. Books covered one of the walls entirely from top to bottom. "You may borrow any of these books during your research here, if you wish. The archive, further down the hall, will be accessible to you also, as it houses past catalogues of all the artists we have on display in the museum. And anything else you might require, please do ask." Then, Lydia formally logged

Emma in as a student and issued her with an identification pass and lanyard; making her now a fully-fledged mature art student.

Eager to recapture student life, Emma selected the books she wished to work from and also requested additional volumes of catalogues from the archive. The first half of that day was spent reading and making notes; with just a short break for coffee and a half hour for lunch. Lydia suggested she should immerse herself in the actual paintings and to spend the afternoon among the masterpieces. It was perfect advice, as her eyes were beginning to tire from staring at books and a computer screen all morning. As it was a Monday, the museum was closed to paying visitors, therefore, Emma had all the gallery rooms to herself to explore in her own time. What bliss! She was drawn immediately to the room housing Klimt's paintings. Instinct had guided her. Completely on her own, she once more gazed up at the golden-haloed lovers in 'The Kiss'. It never failed to bewitch her. The enchantment of the story they portrayed with their passion reflected in the brightness of their robes; was always breath taking!

Each day for two weeks, Emma followed the same routine with only a break at weekends to shop for wedding attire with Alice. They had discovered an independent dress boutique tucked away in a side street; with a poster advertising a winter sale pasted across its window. Alice had tried on a romantic white, Empire style dress with a long, flowing chiffon skirt and fitted bodice; she had felt like Empress Sisi, the wife of Emperor Franz Joseph, as soon as she had put it on and had twirled in front of the mirror. This would have been the perfect dress but because Karl hadn't yet had any luck being able to book a venue, and time was running out to find anywhere available, Alice had been reluctant to buy it. They were becoming despondent and were visualising having to postpone their wedding plans when Emma suddenly had a brainwave: "I've just had a brilliant idea! What about The Belvedere as your venue? It would be the ideal setting for a romantic New Year/Millennium wedding. Of course, I would need to ask Lydia, but I do believe there *is* a party arranged for that night. Fingers crossed they'll agree." She stated at the same time enthusiastically crossing her own fingers.

Eagerly the following Monday morning, Emma headed straight to Lydia's office and from her heart, poured out her suggestion. She briefly explained the significance of her friend's urgency to be married and all the travails she had overcome; hoping this would gain sympathy and agree to her request. It had worked. Lydia was sympathetic but said she would need to contact the head of events at the museum for it to be formally agreed. Emma was in the archive, looking at sketches Klimt had drawn of Emilie during the years 1902-1909 as she was fascinated by their relationship. This was where Lydia had found her to impart the good news she had hoped for.

"Thank you so much. My friends will be delighted and grateful for your kindness. They will be so thrilled!" She felt like hugging Lydia but knew this would be vastly inappropriate.

On Christmas Eve, Emma and Gustav with Alice and Karl went to Midnight Mass along with the majority of the population of the city. It was the one night the churches throughout the country could guarantee a full house. They joined a candle-lit procession that snaked its way through the crisp, cold air with the sound of footsteps crunching the packed snow. It looked like a scene from a Christmas tableau. People were in a festive mood as they had eaten their traditional Christmas fare of fried carp and were looking forward to opening their presents back home after the service. Emma and Alice thought it strange as the opening of gifts was normally designated to Christmas Day for them, but when in Rome, as the saying goes. They had all been invited to Frederik's house the following day to continue the festivities. Emma had ordered and purchased a large Sacher torte to take with. She knew this would be appreciated as they were very much a food-conscious family; better than another bauble to gather dust, she had decided. Gustav along with his mother, Mrs Katz, had also been invited, mainly as a thank you for their kindness in making Emma feel included, but also as they were friends of the family. The day had been spent eating good food and laughing; whereas the ones at home were just overeating and watching telly, and she knew she will miss this feeling of being surrounded by fun and friendship.

That night, Gustav walked her back to the house, whilst the others had taken taxis as they all had had plenty to drink. He had given her a pale blue, cashmere hat and scarf set when they had exchanged gifts earlier. Emma had felt guilty as all she had bought him was a Klimt China mug from The Belvedere's gift shop. But he had looked delighted when he had opened it; or had at least pretended to. Well wrapped up in their thick duvet style coats, they held hands as they made the short walk back with the bright moonlight behind them. Their shadows cast in front as if they were being guided by elongated giants. Before going in, he hesitated and turned to tilt her chin up to meet his lips. She didn't object and the kiss became urgently stronger. He parted her lips with his smooth, wet tongue, exploring her inner mouth before locking with her own compliant one, as if mating. The door suddenly opening jolted them apart and Mrs Katz began calling for her cat.

Chapter Fifty

Her student days were coming to a close as this was the last week, for now anyway, of her sojourn in Vienna. It had flown by. Christmas was over and Gustav had gone to stay with friends, promising he would return before the wedding. So, the hopes of a romantic liaison had been abandoned. Her studying had gone well and she had learned a great deal; and had ticked off most of the subject requests on Charles' list. Now, she only had a few days left to complete that list and to assist Alice and Karl in their wedding preparations. They had been overjoyed when she had told them that their wedding could go ahead and Karl had managed to book a registrar; with much bribing of champagne and canopies at the celebratory party afterwards. All Alice needed to do was buy the dress she had tried on, and had fallen in love with; praying it was still for sale. However, when her and Emma, went there, the shop had been closed and the shutters had been firmly down. The sign on the door stated that 'this shop will re-open on 2 January 2000' and apologised too for any inconvenience this might cause.

"It had probably been closed all over the Christmas holidays and had decided to extend it to after the New Year." Emma said after reading it out loud to a disheartened Alice who was on the verge of tears.

"Where will I find another one? I had set my *heart* on that dress. I should have bought it when I had the chance." She said furiously and stamped the ground like a misbehaved child. Trying to placate her with promises of finding another equally, if not more beautiful dress, Emma was secretly stumped to know where. Downheartedly, they made their way back by tram to Karl's flat. They had only been in ten minutes before Karl came home.

"Why are you so glum?" He asked Alice. "We will be getting married in a few days, you should be feeling excited and happy."

"If I don't have anything to wear, how will we be married?" And she explained the closure of the shop. He shrugged his shoulders in response and left the room. "He wouldn't care even if I turned up in an old jogging suit. Men haven't a clue!"

"Really?" He said, walking in carrying a large box in both arms. "This is my wedding present to you." And he placed it by the side of her chair. Intrigued, she opened the lid and gasped. Nestled inside was her beautiful dress. "But they were closed?" She questioned. He told her he had bought it the next day after she had first tried it on. He knew she had wanted it so much.

"You are the best husband to be and I can't wait to marry you!" At last, Alice had a beaming smile on her face. "Now all we have to do is get the perfect dress for you to wear." She said looking at Emma.

The Belvedere Events personnel were frantically carrying out the plans that had been made since the summer for a spectacular party to welcome in the year 2000. With only two days to go to the big event, a marquee was currently being erected in the gardens near to the foyer. Five hundred people of the great and good of Viennese society, had received their invitations a month previously, and at a price of 250 euros a ticket, only the well-heeled could afford the cost. The staff, including volunteers, with their families had been given complimentary passes as an appreciation for their work throughout the past year.

Alice and Karl's wedding ceremony had been organised to take place before any of the guests would have arrived for the main party. Theirs would be an intimate gathering of their own family and friends, but they would also be expected to stay for the entire night's celebrations. It was planned to be the most spectacular event that night in Vienna and in the modern age of The Belvedere. More than on any other New Year's Eve had the stores, selling exclusive gowns, been inundated by frantic purchasing. Dress racks had been depleted by wealthy customers almost coming to blows over each garment; likening it to no better than on a high-class market stall. Amongst this melee, Emma knew she would have a problem finding something suitable to wear. As the chief bridesmaid, even though she was the only one, her outfit had to suit the occasion and the setting. With this in mind, Emma consulted Lydia about her growing idea.

"I wonder, Lydia, does the museum have a costumes department?" She had asked on locating her in the foyer looking out on the transformation of the site before her.

"Yes, we do. It is in the basement and a conservator regularly inspects the collection for any sign of damage due to humidity or infestation." She explained authoritatively to Emma. "They are usually displayed alongside the artwork of the period that is being exhibited."

Excitedly, Emma asked if it would be possible to venture down there to see the collection. In her mind, she knew what she was looking for. And so, Lydia kindly arranged a time slot for Emma to be accompanied into the basement for that afternoon. The costumes had been classified into groups from the various eras and relating to the country of birth of each artist, hence an array of traditional costumes. In this section, which Emma was able to look through were all copies of the real attire that had been worn in their day; the genuine articles were stowed away wrapped in acid-proof tissue paper and kept in an environmentally controlled temperature. No one other than a curator would be allowed, without supervision, to handle them, she had been told. The dress she was searching for had been worn by Emilie Flöge when she had posed for Klimt around 1902/03. There had been so many to choose from, but this one had stood out in her mind. At last, she had found it! Emilie had looked stunning in it and she, Emma, wanted to emulate that image. The iridescent blues and turquoise were offset with snaking geometric patterns in gold and brown along the length of the dress and the full puffed sleeve came into a wide cuff at the wrist. Yes, this was the one, most definitely! Thankfully, these costumes were able to be hired out, as they were usually lent to theatrical companies; giving the museum an additional small income. Carrying her prized possession back to Lydia's office, she had it booked out under Emma's name.

"But I won't take it away with me now." She had stated to Lydia. "Would it be all right to leave it here, for safety until the big day?" Agreeing with Emma, as Lydia had preferred that arrangement, she quickly locked it away in a spare locker and gave the key to Emma.

The remainder of that afternoon, Emma dreamily imagined herself wearing that stunning dress and feeling like she belonged in an oil painting. All she told Alice when she arrived at their flat that evening was that she had found her own perfect dress for the wedding. When asked what it was like, she hadn't wanted to describe it; a description wouldn't have done it justice and would have spoiled the surprise. As it was bitter cold outside, Karl offered to drive her back to Mrs Katz's house. It was on his way, he had said, as he was picking up a fare at the Christmas market in The Schönbrunn Palace courtyard. There was a lot of work to be had in December as soon as the festive markets came to the city; tourists arrived from around the world to spend long weekends soaking up the atmosphere and traditionally getting merry on glöwhein, which in turn made all the taxi drivers equally merry knowing their profits will be boosted and their own Christmases will be full and plenty.

Emma had been given her own key to the front door when she had first arrived. She had just put the key in the lock when the door opened before she had even turned it. Gustav had returned. "I promised I would come back before the wedding. I have been waiting for you." He looked pleased with himself like the cat with the proverbial cream. This annoyed Emma. *Cheek! If he thinks I'll run into his arms now like a good little girl, he's going to be disappointed*, she thought. "Good night!" and walked past him and ascended the stairs to her room. That will teach him to take me for granted and she smiled at her own self-assurance.

Before she had left work earlier, she had searched through her collection of books and catalogue raisonné on Gustav Klimt, looking for that one image of Emilie wearing *her* dress. After she had found it, she had taken it to be photocopied, so that she would now be able to prop it up on the chest of drawers and gaze at it imagining it to be her. And that's how she fell asleep; hypnotised with images of that dress dancing in the arms of an unknown.

Chapter Fifty-One

She awoke realising this would be her penultimate day studying at The Belvedere. She had enjoyed every minute of it and the entire experience had been invaluable for her career. Today, she had planned to complete the last item on the list; the full study of Klimt's most famous oil painting 'The Kiss'. *They say leave the best to last.* And this is what she had done. She had studied all his other fine works in the gallery; spending almost a day on each one, taking numerous notes and photographs. But at the end of each afternoon, she would make a point of visiting this special masterpiece before leaving for the day. It never failed to inspire her imagination. She would talk to it openly. Telling the characters, the lovers in their intimate embrace, how lucky they were to have each other. Perhaps, they could hear her; she imagined they could and once she thought she saw Emilie's eyes flicker in response. She had felt a connection.

There hadn't been any sign of Gustav's presence in the house before she had left for the museum. She had gulped down a quick cup of coffee and a pastry at Mrs Katz insistence, then dashed out of the door, pre-empting any awkward questioning concerning her son. The tram seemed busier than ever, swallowing up commuters and shoppers alike in its wake before spitting them out at their various destinations. There was already an expectant feel in the air as the dawning of a new millennium, a new age, approached ever nearer. There had been rumours that technical equipment would become dysfunctional and all electrical clocks would turn to zero. No one knew what would happen and that seemed to add to the excitement and anticipation of nearing the end of 1999. Just one more day to go and the world will discover the truth.

The Belvedere was looking magnificent. The decorations were almost completed with the foyer decked out in pine branches with lilac, white and silver ribboning entwined. Balloons of the same colour were grouped tastefully at the entrance; with pine cones and white flower arrangements of gardenias and carnations attached to the balustrades. The pine aroma combined with the scent of the flowers proved an olfactory delight. The pristinely white marquee stood proudly adjacent to the foyer with their internal decorations matching perfectly. The design company, hired for this prestigious occasion, had outdone themselves; they knew they would receive many enquiries for further business and had made certain the overall effect would be superb.

Alice and Karl's wedding ceremony was scheduled for 4 pm inside the marquee, where gas heaters and uplighters would be on at full blast to compensate for the bitterly cold weather outside. This would give them a full hour and a half to celebrate before the main party would begin at 5.30 pm, when guests would be arriving for the reception. A small orchestra will be playing a range of music; anything from Strauss to a variety of up-to-date tunes, throughout the evening and into the night. The climax of the night will culminate in a firework extravaganza that has been set up around the entire gardens and would be seen all over Vienna, at the bewitching hour of 12 am. It promised to be a most memorable night, on all levels.

Emma had been asked to help out in the office with an admin task before going up to the gallery and she felt unable to refuse. Lydia asked her to photocopy the itinerary that was to be handed out to the catering staff so they would be aware of the exact arrival of the guests for the reception to begin along with the canapé and buffet times; everything needed to go to plan for it to be a success. She was pleased to be involved but slightly reluctant to have the time deducted from her own plans. It only took her an hour to complete before she was able to spend the rest of the day as she had wanted. This was the last day the gallery rooms would be open to the public. The museum was scheduled to be closed for the next few days covering the long celebratory weekend and so unfortunately, Emma had to share this last day's studying with other people milling in and out of the gallery. So precious was the time that she didn't want to waste a second. Dismissing any thoughts of lunch, she completely ignored her complaining stomach; consoling it with the promise that she'll eat twice as much tomorrow. Her head was beginning to ache from the concentration of studying the brush strokes on the application of the oils and other more unusual mediums that he had used and was famous for. She had been discreet at taking images at every angle and only using her digital camera when no one else was in the gallery, as photography was disallowed. She remembered Charles had once said to her, "Looking can be a form of worship and accurately observing arouses the imagination." How true these words had come to mean.

She realised it was getting late. The sun was starting to sink slowly in the sky and the remaining visitors were being shown off the premises. It was her cue to stop working and pack away her belongings for the last time. She gave a huge sigh; freeing her body from the gradual build-up of pressure she had dumped on herself knowing this hour would arrive. Looking up at the masterpiece before her she whispered, "I'm not ready to say goodbye. Tomorrow is going to be a most enchanting night and we'll be sharing that magic together." She felt Emilie's response of an electric charge surging through her whole being. Emma was spell-bound.

Hurrying out of The Belvedere, before it closed for the day and the following few days after that, she made her way to the tram stop and hoped she wouldn't have to wait for long. She remembered all the times she had travelled on the same route looking out at the historical buildings along the Ringstrasse and being tempted by the cafés with their selection of pastries on display in their windows. This melancholic feeling lasted all the way back to the boarding house, where Gustav was waiting for her. He threw the cigarette butt on the ground; it sizzled before extinguishing, and a brown stain slowly spread over the hardened snow.

"I am taking you out to dinner tonight and you cannot refuse." He said in a determined no nonsense tone. "You will be gone soon and I would like us to spend some time together." He added. She hadn't the heart to refuse anyway, plus she was very hungry after having skipped her lunch.

"That's fine by me." She replied, and went upstairs to freshen up. They had an enjoyable traditional meal of schnitzel followed by apple strudel and whipped cream. The bottle of red wine they shared relaxed Emma's inhibitions and any thoughts of sadness left her completely. They took a slow walk home as the restaurant hadn't been too far away. He held her round her waist to support her as she kept stumbling on the icy surface; whether it was that or the wine he wasn't sure and didn't care, he was happy just to be with her. And she didn't object when he helped her up the stairs to her room. He picked her up and carried her to her bed where he laid her down gently before removing her shoes. He bent down to kiss her goodnight as he had expected her to turn over, fall asleep and then he would be dismissed. Instead, he was delighted when she unexpectedly flung her arms around his neck and pulled him down towards her. He hesitated in case he was misreading her signals. But she started pulling at his sweater for him to remove it whilst simultaneously removing her own. Her signals became loud and clear! And he definitely wasn't going to refuse her!

Within seconds, their outer clothes had been discarded and had been thrown haphazardly onto the floor. In just their underwear, they immersed themselves underneath the covers, as if hiding from prying eyes. He began kissing her neck and throat and she urged him to remove her bra; urgently assisting him at the same time as the clasp was proving difficult to undo. Her nipples became hard and sensitive to his lips as he rolled them with his tongue, sucking on them like a new-born baby. Emma cried out his name "Gustav, don't stop!" As he entered her, she turned to look at the photograph she had propped up next to the bed. In the throes of ecstasy, she began imagining she was Emilie and Klimt was the real Gustav she was now making love to and whose caresses she was so deliciously responding to. The calibre of the climax confirmed, in her mind, only a person of such greatness could ever make her feel other worldly. And that world was beckoning her.

Chapter Fifty-Two

<u>**Friday, 31 December 1999**</u>
<u>**New Year's Eve – New Millennium Eve**</u>

The dawning of a new era had finally arrived and every person all around the world would remember exactly where they were when they celebrated its entrance.

Emma had a splitting headache; a hangover from an excess of wine from the previous evening. This wasn't how she had envisaged starting the final day of the year, the century, or even the millennium. Her body felt bruised from Gustav's vigorous thrusting between her thighs and from the weight of him when he collapsed on top of her, sated and exhausted. They had fallen asleep with his arms cradling her, but the narrow bed had proved too uncomfortable and she had been aware of a cold draught as he had opened the covers to escape back to his own room in the early hours.

She was pleased that she was now on her own as she could set her plans in motion for the promising day and *night* ahead. The lovemaking had awakened her body and heightened her senses; and by having a refreshing shower, she hoped her headache would give up the ghost and vanish. Unfortunately, the muzziness remained. She had no choice but to ease it further with an intake of water and much coffee; this meant an awkward breakfast facing both the Katz, mother and son. Gustav was already voraciously shovelling scrambled egg and cold sausage into his mouth when Emma made her appearance. Obviously, the appetite he had worked up had needed satisfying and he gave her a boyish grin as if to thank her for the experience. Mrs Katz came in from the kitchen carrying a large pot of freshly made coffee, "I made plenty for your strength, so drink!" She ordered, with a smug, knowing look directed at them both. Emma cringed with embarrassment. The welcoming hot, molten liquid quickly revived her composure and she announced that she would be leaving them today as she had already arranged to stay with Alice and Karl after the wedding, before returning to England. This was a lie as she hadn't pre-planned anything, but she was feeling trapped and had fabricated this on the spur of the moment. She hadn't wanted Gustav to think that they were now an item. He had looked crestfallen and had tried to persuade her to stay longer. To placate him, she agreed for him to accompany her to the wedding, but he would have to meet her at The Belvedere as she needed to help Alice get ready.

"Would you be able to drive me to Alice's as it'll be horrendous getting on a tram with a suitcase?" Emma asked him kindly.

"Of course, that will be my pleasure." He assured her.

She thanked Mrs Katz for her hospitality and said she will see her later at the wedding; as she had been invited alongside Viktor's cousin, Frederik and his family. Gustav graciously dropped Emma at Alice and Karl's apartment and said he would be looking forward to seeing them all later. To Alice's amazement, Emma let out a long sigh of relief once Gustav had gone; deflating her lungs like a pair of bellows.

"What's the matter?" Alice enquired, eager to know more.

"I'll tell you another time, but for now it's your day and I'm here to help make it perfect for you." Emma had said and then explained the presence of her suitcase as Alice had asked if Emma's dress was inside the case. "Don't worry, my dress is waiting for me in a locker at The Belvedere. I'll change into it just before the service."

It's purported to be bad luck for the groom to see his bride-to-be before the ceremony, but Alice and Karl didn't believe in superstition, and as they had nowhere else to get ready but in their own home, they were prepared to take that chance. Emma presented Alice with a tiara that would complement her dress and make her feel like a true princess. She wanted her friend to remember every wonderful detail of her special wedding day and hoped it would be able to cancel out the dreadful ordeal she had been subjected to and leave her only with good, happy memories. With a flourishing display that any sommelier would be proud of, Emma popped the cork of the champagne bottle she had brought with her and filled three glasses:

"To my best friend in the whole world and her soon-to-be husband, I wish you all the happiness in a long and healthy life together." They chinked their glasses in response and hugged each other before sipping at the sparkling wine. Immediately, Alice began sneezing as the bubbles, she claimed, had entered her nose. "You're not supposed to inhale it, Alice." Emma stated, laughing at her friend's attempt to drink and sneeze at the same time.

It was time to leave for their wedding ceremony at The Belvedere. Karl had ordered a special carriage drawn by two horses to take him and Alice there. He was dressed in a black dinner suit with a silver-grey bow tie on a snow-white shirt. Alice told him he looked like James Bond, so suave and handsome, that she couldn't wait to be his wife. He reciprocated by telling her she was the most beautiful woman, his princess, who he will adore forever. They were a handsome couple. The retractable roof of the carriage ensured some degree of warmth and dryness during the ride there and prevented them from also being windswept. The weather had held mercifully, as more snow had been forecast for the following day. As they rode along towards their venue, the display of burnt umber and crimson reds intermingled with cerise pinks that the setting sun was exhibiting, was worthy of any artist's palette. Alice felt like the luckiest girl alive. They alighted outside the foyer; a photographer was there to capture the moment, and this would be just one of many images that would be taken throughout the entire evening and coming night.

Emma had arrived before them in a taxi that Karl had ordered from a close friend of his. Now, she needed to get herself ready. Her fingers began shaking as she held the key to unlock the locker. The anticipation of wearing the dress that will transform herself into her namesake, Emilie, was overpowering. The magical time was nearing. Carefully, she carried it to the staff room where Lydia had said she could change there without being disturbed. Instantly, she put it over her head and wriggled into it she felt complete. The look was perfect. She was now Emilie; the dress flowed to the floor and the wide collar, drawn by a thread, stood up like a halo surrounding her hair that she had curled especially in Emilie's style. Emma had copied every minute detail of the picture she cherished so much. The first step of her plan had been completed, now she could put the rest in motion.

4 pm The Wedding Ceremony

All the guests for the wedding were waiting excitedly inside the marquee for Alice and Karl to arrive. A hush came over the gathering as they heard the clip-clop of the horses' hooves come to a standstill outside. They were greeted by a round of applause as they entered the venue. Emma followed them in carrying a posy of white gardenias interspersed with green fern and gypsophila that Alice had handed to her. "Emma, you look amazing, just like the picture you showed me." Alice smiled, realising now why Emma had been so secretive.

"You look pretty wonderful yourself." Her friend replied with choked up emotion.

Karl's dad was proudly sporting a white carnation buttonhole and his mum a corsage of the same flowers; proud parents who had longed for this day. The service began promptly and the registrar spoke in English for Alice's benefit and then translated each sentence into Austrian for the congregation. After they had exchanged their vows and rings, a chorus of congratulations could be heard from various denominations, including a smattering of 'Mazel Tov' from Frederik's family. Many photographs were taken and the cutting of the cake was observed to the delight of Karl's mum who had spent a week making and icing it to perfection. Everyone was jolly and already in a party mood as the majority of guests began to arrive for the main event: The New Year's/Millennium Eve Party.

5.30-6 pm Reception and Canapés

Lydia was at the entrance to the foyer with a list on a clipboard of all the guests they were expecting to arrive; their names received a tick by the side of each one after the presentation of their invitation. She had been pleased by the overwhelming positive response to the elaborate decorations the building and gardens had received especially for the occasion: 'a glittering display of snow white, light purple and sparkling silver fit for a Hans Christian Anderson fable production', one over-excited guest had remarked. Now they had all arrived, the catering staff had been busy circulating with hot canapés as a precursor to the main buffet. Most of the guests remained inside the comparative warmth of the marquee. Just a few couples ventured outside to admire the decorated gardens with the fountains lit up in the same themed colours of the night; of these, the wealthiest ladies used this to flaunt their expensive fur coats of mink, ermine or any another poor animal bred entirely to adorn the backs of the privileged. It had made Emma's skin crawl to see some of them with the deflated body of the animal wrapped around their shoulders with the lifeless head and legs dangling uselessly when once it would have been chasing gloriously through fields and streams.

Gustav hadn't had a chance to talk with Emma and had been searching for her amongst the crowd inside the marquee. He finally found her outside with Lydia. Her dress had surpassed all others and he wanted to tell her that.

"You look stunning, a definite homage to Emilie Flöge! You have embodied her magnificently." He had become breathless with admiration.

"Thank you, that was the idea I was aiming for." She replied a little irritated. *After all, he wasn't the Gustav, she wanted to impress, hopefully that will be soon,* she thought to herself.

7-9.30 pm Buffet Dinner

The master of ceremonies announced for all the guests to be seated at their tables and hoped everyone had studied the elaborate, hand-painted table plan which was on an easel, displayed at the entrance. There followed a low murmur, like bees buzzing, as people scurried to find their allocated table each designated with a miniature framed picture of a famous work of art. Klimt's 'The Kiss' had been reserved for Emma and the wedding party. Lydia had overseen this detail much to Emma's satisfaction. The small orchestra situated at the far end of the pavilion that had been warming up during the reception, now began to play gentle arias from Strauss to enhance the atmosphere.

Each table was called up individually to be served by professional, smartly attired waitresses in traditional black skirts with white blouses and frilly white aprons; ensuring there would be plenty of food for everyone and without a panic ensuing. It hadn't taken long before the beautiful white damask-linen table cloths became stained with blotches of red wine and dark brown gravy marks. Fortuitously, the candelabras held battery lights and were not dripping wax onto the cloths from real candles. Tall and elegant, glass vases half-filled with a light purple coloured water, central to each round table, held a floral display with balloons attached; just high enough to allow conversation without being distracted by foliage. The catering company had certainly exceeded their remit.

Emma was too nervous to eat and had only picked at the food on her plate. She looked over at Alice and Karl who were beaming with happiness. A warm glow spread through Emma to see her loyal friend deliriously happy. She had earned that happiness, no, deserved it with everything she had done unconditionally for Emma. She loved her but knew it was soon time to find her own happiness. Excusing herself by saying she needed the bathroom, she left them all eating and chattering, with the volume gradually becoming higher so as to be heard above the general hullabaloo.

10-11 pm Dancing Begins

2 Hours to Midnight

She had managed to escape. Emma had hurried out of the marquee before anyone had noticed and aimed for the stairs leading to the galleries.

The orchestra had begun playing a variety of more modern tunes suitable for all ages to dance to; with the sound of scraping back of chairs on the temporary wooden flooring, men were escorting their partners to join them in variations of movements associated with dancing. The laughter and high spirits rang out in the cold night air, echoing round the gardens as if there were loud-speakers in every corner; an excellent cover for Emma's plans to continue. Again, Gustav was unable to find Emma to dance with, and had felt obliged to ask an unattached cousin of Frederik's to dance with him instead.

Emma headed straight to *her* painting; this is how she thought of it now. Without any overhead lighting to guide her and only the individual spotlights illuminating the artworks to prevent complete darkness, the atmosphere became electric and the enchantment almost complete. She just needed to feel if there would be a reaction to her likeness to Emilie. It was uncanny; she knew she had captured her persona perfectly.

"Just two more hours and I will be with you." She whispered as she looked up and witnessed Emilie's smile.

From the gallery, she tiptoed back down to the staff room where she had left her belongings. So sure was she now of what the outcome will be, she began to write her farewell letters. She retrieved the sheets of stationery she had kept especially for this purpose. Taking her pen, she unfolded the paper and began writing: First one to Viktor who had helped her on this journey and had given her so much; not only entrusting his sketch with her, but the kindness and generosity he always gave to her even when things went horribly wrong.

Then, the second one she wrote to Charles, mainly to thank him for her promotion and for enabling herself to study at such a fine establishment as The Belvedere. Without this, she wouldn't have been able to become so close to her own nirvana. Hopefully, he would find love again as he was too nice a person to be on his own indefinitely.

The third letter was to Alice, her dearest friend. She hoped she would understand in time the reasoning behind her momentous action and forgive her for deserting her. She wished her and Karl a long and happy life together and if one day, they were lucky enough to have a daughter, please would they name her Emma; after her crazy 'auntie' who proved you *can* fulfil your dreams.

The last letter was to her dear, dear mother. This was the saddest one of all. Knowing she would not be there to help and comfort her as she became older, gave Emma an intense pang of guilt. Try to be happy for me, Mum, even though I won't be back with you, take comfort in knowing I'll be so very happy living a new life; one I have been destined for. I will love you eternally and thank you for giving me life. Emma x

Each letter she carefully folded and placed them inside an envelope, marking them individually with their names and addresses. She then tucked them all into a larger envelope with an attached note requesting for them to be posted as soon as possible, but apologising for not leaving any money for their postage. On this one, Emma wrote Lydia's name and underlined it several times and wrote the word 'URGENT' in the top right-hand corner. Satisfied, that she had completed her objective, she placed this envelope inside Lydia's pigeon-hole where she expected it would remain until the museum's re-opening on 2 January 2000.

11 pm (One Hour to Midnight)

The dance floor was heaving under the weight of a lengthy conger-line formation that was being added to as it snaked its way around each abandoned table looking like a centipede with legs kicking out to the rhythm. By this time, Emma could see the majority of guests were intoxicated by alcohol and had discarded their inhibitions; the immaculate hairdos had become dishevelled with fine gold combs and other hair adornments littering the floor, resembling a Magpie's nest. Shoes had been kicked off haphazardly making Emma wonder how the owners would manage to find a matching pair at the end of the night. Deep with this thought, she suddenly found herself being dragged by the arm to join Gustav, Alice and Karl in the festivities.

"Come on, party pooper, you've been gone ages." Alice shouted to be heard above the music. "Join in the fun!"

Laughing with the others, Emma relaxed, determined to make this last hour before midnight a memorable one. One her friends will recall when they are reminiscing about her in years to come.

An announcement came from the orchestra's conductor that they will be slowing the pace down to allow the waiters to fill champagne glasses in readiness for the approaching bewitching hour, and would all guests please return to their tables. Determined to have one last dance with Emma, Gustav pulled her close to him and begun swaying with her in time to the melody. He began whispering his affections as he kissed her hair and then her cheek, and telling her how beautiful she looked. Steeling herself, she quickly turned her head before he could reach her lips. "Please, Gustav, it's no use!" She pulled away from him and sat with the others at the table. Disgruntled, he followed her and sat down next to her.

"Why? What have I done wrong?" He pleaded, confused at her coldness towards him.

"Please, don't spoil the night," she said trying to placate him. "We'll talk about it another time."

He accepted her answer and hoped this meant she would be agreeable to his charms much later when they will be together in the early hours of a new year.

11.50 pm (Ten Minutes to Midnight)

Everyone's glasses were charged with champagne. The orchestra had stopped playing. The anticipated countdown would soon begin. The master of ceremonies made an announcement for all guests who wished to witness the spectacular firework display, to make their way outside as it would be starting at the stroke of midnight. Excitedly, people scattered in all directions to claim their coats, fur wraps, cloaks and any other outer garments they had discarded at the beginning of the evening. The icy-cold wintry night air greeted them as they poured out of the marquee, and into the gardens. The jollity suddenly halted as the transition from the warm interior suddenly took effect. Anticipating this, blazing braziers had been lit in regular intervals to help combat any discomfort. Appreciating the thoughtfulness of the organisers, the crowd quickly relaxed and resumed their laughter; exhaling clouds of vapours as if they were dragons breathing out dissipated fire.

11.55 pm (Five Minutes to Midnight)

Emma together with Alice, Karl and the rest of the wedding party joined everyone else, standing outside in the bitter cold. Karl held Alice close to him to keep her warm while the others gathered round a brazier, and getting as close to it as possible without being scorched.

"You're shivering, Emma!" Alice concerned for her friend stated she should borrow her thick, white velvet cloak lined with rabbit fur.

"Then, you'll be cold, silly." Emma laughingly replied between her chattering teeth. "I left my coat in Lydia's office by mistake. I'll go and fetch it. I won't be long. But just in case I don't get back in time, Happy New Year and Happy New Millennium to you all!" She gave Alice a big hug that lasted a few seconds squeezing her hard, and then blew kisses for everyone else.

"Surely, you'll be back by then if you go quickly?" Alice quizzically replied feeling slightly alarmed at Emma's strange words.

Unable to reply for fear of letting her guard down, Emma smiled at Alice and mouthed the words "I love you, Goodbye," and rushed off into the building. Alice watched as she weaved in and out of the throng until she saw the beautiful iridescent blues and turquoise of her dress disappear forever. A heavy sadness had crept up through her body until it reached her heart and she knew somehow that she would never see her friend again. Karl sensed the change in Alice, "What is wrong? You cannot look sad on our wedding day."

Alice just shrugged and hoped she would be proven completely wrong; an over-reaction, I'll laugh with Emma about it tomorrow. She said trying to convince herself.

Midnight 12 am

Instead of collecting her coat, Emma was mounting the staircase leading up to the galleries. The countdown had begun. She could hear the crowd outside excitedly shouting down the seconds. I must get there before they reach the end.
10...9...8...7...6...5...4...3...2...1

At the last second, Emma stood staring up at her painting; transfixed, just as she was the very first time she had seen it. An explosion of fireworks rocked the skies, illuminating the gallery with showers of gold, purples, greens and blues as rockets flew amongst the stars; as if Klimt himself had opened his palette and was painting the scene.

"I am here." She said, to the background of clocks all over the city striking the magical hour. Gazing directly into Emilie's eyes, Emma felt her warmth engulf her. "I *am* ready, now!" She spoke out.

Emilie Flöge turned her bewitching smile towards Emma. Emilie had been waiting a long time for this moment. Her earthly body had died in 1952 at the same time Emma's mother had been born. The connection between them ensured that when a daughter was born, unbeknownst, she would carry her name as she was destined, one day, to receive her spirit.

Reaching out her arms, Emma felt a strong force pulling at her entire being. She closed her eyes to concentrate fully on her body being transformed into Emilie's; Emilie's spirit entering hers. For a moment, between the transitioning, she was made aware of an alarm ringing somewhere. Of course, she thought, I've set the painting's alarm system off, never mind, the fireworks will muffle the sound. Those were her last thoughts as Emma Louise Fogle became Emilie Louise Flöge; Gustav Klimt's lover.

This is now the start of my new life and the beginning of a great love story.

Epilogue

Dear Charles,

By the time you would receive this letter, you will have realised that I won't be returning, so sorry. Thank you so much for offering me my job back and giving me a second chance. I want you to know I was happy working with you at the gallery, but my life has now taken an unexpected turn and…I'm ecstatic!

I always knew Vienna was a magical city containing the spirits of long-ago talented artists and musicians. And I reached out to them or should I say, one in particular, and he returned my touch. I am sure you know who I mean.

Viktor maintained I had a likeness, a similarity to Emilie Louise Flöge, not only in name, but in looks. *I belong to that time! I was her!* The feelings of déja vu occurred too often not to realise the connection; Emilie died in 1952, the very same year my mother was born. Was this a mere coincidence or reincarnation? It cannot be proven, only embraced. And I am now embracing it with all my heart and soul.

I hope, Charles, your life becomes more settled. Perhaps, once Dominic fully recovers, and I hope for your sake he does, he will progress to being a brother you can trust and love. Don't hold grudges, life is too short! Make amends, as he is the only family you have.

Think of me when you have a spare moment and try to believe that it is me you are seeing each time you gaze up at Klimt's 'The Kiss'. It will be!

Goodbye forever, Charles,
Emma (Emilie).

PS If you intend to keep my sketch, please look after it always and perhaps offer Viktor a substantial recompense for it in my name. x

Book Two
EMILIE

The whooshing sound in my ears subsided as soon as I entered her body; my spirit settled comfortably like an old glove and the transition became complete. The sensation of a floating weightlessness and being surrounded in a dazzling white light gave way to a calm serenity. I had become Emilie.

Although my future is set in the past, I know it is complicated to understand, but I had been born for this!

Author's Note

All the characters in my story are fiction. Gustav Klimt and Emilie Flöge were lifelong friends; whether they were lovers has been open for debate among art historians for many years. Gustav Klimt had made many sketches throughout his illustrious life as an artist, but this one depicted at the centre of my story is entirely fictional.

I hope you have enjoyed reading this book and will look forward to reading its prequel: EMILIE, of which the first paragraph has been included to whet your imagination.